ETHAN MARCUS

MAKES HIS MARK

TAKE A STAND!

Ethan Marcus Stands Up

Ethan Marcus Makes His Mark

ETHAN MARCUS MAKES HIS MARK

WITHDRAWN

BY MICHELE WEBER HURWITZ

ALADDIN

New York London Toronto Sydney New Delhi

ALADDIN

An imprint of Simon & Schuster Children's Publishing Division

1230 Avenue of the Americas, New York, New York 10020

First Aladdin paperback edition November 2019

Text copyright © 2018 by Michele Weber Hurwitz

Cover illustration copyright © 2018 by Hugo Santos

Also available in an Aladdin hardcover edition.

All rights reserved, including the right of reproduction in whole or in part in any form.

ALADDIN and related logo are registered trademarks of Simon & Schuster, Inc.

For information about special discounts for bulk purchases, please contact Simon & Schuster Special Sales at 1-866-506-1949 or business@simonandschuster.com.

The Simon & Schuster Speakers Bureau can bring authors to your live event. For more information or to book an event contact the Simon & Schuster Speakers Bureau at 1-866-248-3049 or visit our website at www.simonspeakers.com.

Book designed by Laura Lyn DiSiena

The text of this book was set in Miller Text.

Manufactured in the United States of America 1019 OFF

10 9 8 7 6 5 4 3 2 1

Library of Congress Control Number 2018957209

ISBN 978-1-4814-8928-7 (hc)

ISBN 978-1-4814-8929-4 (pbk)

ISBN 978-1-4814-8930-0 (eBook)

To my four compass points, who
always steer me in the right direction:
Ben, Rachel, Sam, and Cassie

ETHAN MARCUS

MAKES HIS MARK

CHAPTER ONE

Frankenstorm

ETHAN

As worst days go, the Monday after Thanksgiving break is right up there with the last day of summer vacation. Not as bad, I'll give you that. But hear me out. The alarm goes off at seven fifteen. You jolt awake, and then three sad facts slowly materialize in your brain: (1) The little party you had going on in the family room with constant televised sports and unlimited snacks is over. (2) Three months of winter are ahead. No more wearing shorts, shooting baskets on the driveway, or going outside without a jacket. And (3) School. You have to go back.

Enough said? Yeah, I thought so.

On top of that, you're still recovering from Thanksgiving itself. The stuffing-related stomachache, your relatives interrogating you, and having to sit next to Grandpa Jerome, who kept yelling "WHAT?" while spitting half-chewed turkey on your arm. Luckily, you had a fancy cloth napkin to use as a shield.

Unfortunately for me, today is that Monday.

I drag myself out of bed and grab a T-shirt and jeans from the pile of clothes on my beanbag, then go downstairs to the kitchen, where my sister, Erin, is spreading peanut butter on a piece of toast. Perfectly even, making sure to completely cover each corner.

She sighs. "I thought this day would never come. I'm so happy to be going back to school. Being home gets really old after a while."

I make a grumble/growl noise because words are just too much effort at the moment.

She cuts her toast into six equal squares, then pops one into her mouth. She chews it exactly five times before swallowing. She's very precise about chewing. And everything else.

I stumble to the cabinet, take out a bowl, plunk it on the counter.

"I'm so excited to start the historical-fiction unit in language arts," Erin says. "I heard we get to dress up as our favorite character at the end. How fun will that be?"

I get the cereal, milk, a spoon. "I can't think of anything I want to do more."

She rolls her eyes, then smiles. "Oh, Ethan."

Erin's only eleven months older than me, and we're both in seventh grade, but she's sounding more and more like Mom every day. This is not good on a lot of levels.

I stand at the counter, hunch over my bowl, start eating.

Erin finishes her toast, then rinses the dish and knife and puts them into the dishwasher. She hoists her backpack onto a stool and rifles through it. "Wow, this is *so* unlike me. Good thing I checked. I almost forgot my mechanical pencil! I think I left it in my room. Be back in a sec." She runs out of the kitchen.

I keep eating my cereal, but even Cheerios aren't cheering me up.

When Erin comes back, I ask, "Where's Mom?" Dad leaves for work at five a.m., so he's never around in the morning, but Mom usually is.

"She had to run out early for a staff meeting. I assured her we'd lock up." Erin glances at me. "You better get moving. The bus will be here in . . ." She checks the time on her phone because she doesn't trust the clock on the microwave. "Ten minutes."

I scoop up the last soggy circle, then put my bowl into the sink.

Erin tilts her head. "Dishwasher."

I groan but open the dishwasher door and put my bowl and spoon inside. After everything that happened with Invention Day a few weeks ago, Erin and I have a different kind of deal going on. A sort of peace-ish treaty. We get how the two of us are day and night and black and white and all that. But that doesn't mean we don't still annoy each other. Fairly frequently.

"Where's your backpack?" she asks.

I look around the kitchen. "Upstairs?"

"Were you planning on getting it anytime soon?"

As I was saying.

A few minutes later I have my backpack and we're out the door, with Erin checking that it's locked about ten times. She even goes, "Okay, okay, the door is locked."

"Yes! It's locked!" I pull her arm. "Let's go."

At the bus stop, most people's eyes are half-closed, and some kids are swaying a little, like they're asleep while standing on the sidewalk. When the bus gets there, I take my usual seat next to Brian Kowalski.

He grunts.

I yawn.

We understand each other perfectly, and have since kindergarten.

People are quiet during the ride, and I know for certain that every single kid on this bus is dreading the first sight of McNutt Junior High. Every kid except one. Erin's in the front row talking to Parneeta, who's definitely asleep. Eyes closed, head plastered to the window, mouth slightly open. But that doesn't stop Erin from describing in great detail the "supposedly riveting" historical-fiction book we're going to read in LA.

Too soon, it's 8:20 a.m., first period, and I'm in math with my butt planted in a chair. Mrs. Genovese peers at us through her giant round owl glasses and grins. "Welcome back, everyone!" She gestures to the whiteboard. "Let's get right down to work. Go ahead and start the warm-up problems. I hope your brains aren't still full of turkey!"

Mine obviously is. I forgot my pencil case in my

locker and have to raise my hand to ask for a pencil. Mrs. Genovese has an emergency stash for people like me. Nice, but if you don't return the pencil, sharpened, at the end of class, she writes your name in a little notebook. It affects your grade in some way. It's happened. I've heard.

She hands me a pencil, and I stare at the first problem. I've also forgotten how to do any kind of equation. How many days until winter break? Fifteen. Correction: fifteen long, boring, scoma-inducing seven-hour days of school.

Yeah, I'm still having scomas. Scoma = school-coma, in case you forgot. After making the desk-evator for Invention Day, I had high hopes. The concept was brilliant—it really was. Even if the prototype was made from spatulas, chip clips, a broken cutting board, and an entire roll of duct tape. Don't ask.

My plan—my dream—was that kids would clip it onto their desks and be able to stand up in class when they needed to stretch their legs and defog their brains. It didn't win or anything, but afterward, Erin got people to do a serious protest in LA about how long we have to sit in school. The protest was amazing—everyone did it! We've—uh, she's—been working on a report about the benefits of standing desks, and we're going to present it to Mrs. D'Antonio, the principal, but until then my butt remains sadly in my seat.

I was sure I'd be scoma-free by now, but Erin says there are a lot of "facts and figures" to "compile" and she's been "really busy." Busy with what, you want to know? Busy being Erin.

I squint at the whiteboard and try to remember what a polynomial is, then look out the window for help. Sometimes that works. Like the sun pierces my brain or something. But instead I see something better than help. A big, fat snowflake drifting past the glass.

A minute later I spot a second one. Then a third, a fourth, and, suddenly, a bunch more falling from the whitish-gray sky.

This is good. Definitely good.

A blizzard is supposed to hit some parts of the Midwest today. The weather people are calling it Frankenstorm. But last night Mom and Dad weren't buying it. Dad packed up his work papers like usual. "They often blow these things out of proportion," he said. Mom agreed and told us to plan on going to school since it hadn't been canceled.

Mom and Dad are not panicky-type people. They always stick to their Parenting 101 philosophy: stay calm, be patient, and let your kids make their own choices. Except, apparently, in the case of snow predictions. Because I would've decided to stay home. You know, just as a precaution.

When math is over, I give Genovese the pencil so she won't write my name in her pencil-criminal notebook, and then I go to social studies. It keeps snowing. Science. More snow. By now nobody's concentrating or even listening. The view out the window is hypnotizing us.

People are whispering and sneak-texting under their desks. A rumor starts floating around about an early dismissal. And another rumor that tests are going to be moved back and homework deadlines will be extended.

In Spanish, Señora Pling is more jittery than usual, her bracelets jangling wildly as she sweeps her arm toward the window, shouting, *"¿Qué pasa?"*

Then the best rumor of all hits the McNutt hallways:

not only an early dismissal, but a possible snow day tomorrow. Everyone's saying it's supposed to keep snowing all night. I hear eight inches. Ten. Twenty! A hundred!

Zoe Feld-Kramer, Erin's best friend, rushes up to me as I'm walking into the cafeteria for lunch. She grabs my hand and squeezes it because I think she thinks we're going out. "Maybe if there's a snow day, we can have plans!" she says. "Hang out? Do something fun?"

I clear my throat. "Uh . . . maybe."

She zooms toward the table where she sits with Erin and the rest of their friends.

At Invention Day, Zoe kissed me. Yes, on the lips. We went to a movie once. Just her and me. It was a dumb movie and Dad drove us and the whole deal was really awkward, and now I have no idea about anything.

"Marcus!" Brian calls, waving at me. "Get over here!"

I haven't even unwrapped my sandwich when Mrs. D'Antonio's voice crackles over the loudspeaker. "May I have your attention please?"

The cafeteria is 100 percent silent. People are holding their water bottles in mid-drink. Forks and spoons are down; eyes are wide. No one's even blinking. It's like a sitting freeze dance.

"Due to the snow, we will be dismissing . . ."

And it's official. We're getting out of here at two p.m. Mrs. D says more, but I can't hear because the cafeteria more or less explodes. The guys at my table stand and applaud. The theater table starts singing a song from *Wicked*, I think. The people at the popular-kid table are taking pictures and immediately posting them (#mcnuttearlydismissal, of course). Brian throws his banana high into the air, then catches it behind his back with one hand. Mrs. Hinkley points at him and blows her whistle. She's blowing her whistle at everyone.

I want to jump and high-five the cafeteria window, but Hinkley'll nail me. So I shout, "Thank you, Frankenstorm!" For saving my sad, scomatized butt and turning an absolute worst day into an absolute best day.

ERIN

This is terrible.

I know, okay? I know what you're thinking. How could I not be happy about an early dismissal and potential snow day? The thing is, and maybe I'm in the minority here, but I like school. Actually, I *love* school, and I'm not embarrassed about saying it. Always have, always will.

Each year, when I tear open the new school-supply pack Mom orders from the PTO, I'm in heaven. There's nothing in the world like six beautiful blank spiral notebooks and the anticipation of filling them with my neat, organized notes all year long. The scent of the clean, fresh paper gets me every time! I use index cards too— for studying and review—and thankfully, a package of five hundred is always included in the box.

I was *so* looking forward to discussing the periodic table in science. I studied it all during break, so I was well prepared. And in LA, Mr. Delman was going to distribute the new novel and read the first chapter aloud. We were supposed to begin talking about point of view and fact versus opinion!

But instead, at 2:01 p.m., what am I doing? Trudging to my locker, putting everything into my backpack, and filing out the back door toward the buses.

Now it'll be another long, slow afternoon at home, trying to find things to do. I was already going stir-crazy over Thanksgiving break. I completed a one-thousand-piece puzzle, watched movies, finished two books, even reorganized all my dresser drawers. And, of course, continued my research for the report on standing desks.

When I have lots of assignments and projects for my classes, my heart just feels happier. If I can get into bed with everything crossed out in my assignment notebook, I know I'll sleep well.

Brian and Ethan are in line at our bus, doing the breaststroke as if they're swimming through the blizzard. I stand behind them, and in a few seconds my hat and backpack straps and jacket are covered with snow.

"We might not make it out alive!" Brian shouts.

Ethan laughs. "Every man for himself!"

My brother picks up a handful of snow and plops it onto Brian's back. Brian whoops, then does the same thing to Ethan. At least the two of them have the sense not to walk home like they usually do. It actually does look kind of bad—I can hardly make out Zoe waiting in her bus line. Still, I don't see why we couldn't have gotten through the last two periods of the day.

I settle into my regular seat behind the driver and

next to Parneeta, who's got a huge smile on her face. "Isn't this excellent?" she says. "As soon as I get home, I'm catching up with all my favorite beauty blogs. There's usually a ton of new posts on Mondays."

I hold my backpack on my lap. "We're going to have to make up what we missed, you know. An extra day in June, I'm sure."

"So? Who cares!"

The bus is louder than normal—everyone's talking and shouting and throwing crumpled wads of paper. The driver, Joe, isn't even telling us to "dial it down a notch" like he usually does. He's singing and drumming his fingers on the steering wheel.

Finally we start moving. My phone buzzes, and I pull it out of my backpack. Text from Zoe: If there's a snow day tomorrow, maybe we can all hang out.

By "all" she means Ethan.

Maybe, I reply.

Maybe?

I should probably review some math problems, I say. And I'm still working on the report for Mrs. D'Antonio.

Erin! Snow days are a gift! You have to do something

fun on a snow day. It's a law. She sends me a bunch of smiling emojis. And snowflakes.

Ha-ha. I'll think about it.

Zoe has decided she's in love with my brother. I told her I'm okay with it, but the truth is, just between you and me, I'm trying but I don't exactly see it. He has some charm, and can be funny in a sloppy-clueless way, and I guess a lot of girls think he's cute. And don't get me wrong, I want my best friend to have some romance in her life. But you can't let love take over everything else. Besides, what do they even have in common? I mean, Zoe's not even focusing on the Be Green Club anymore! That was everything to her prior to the Invention Day kissing incident.

The bus crawls along. What's normally a twenty-minute trip takes twice the amount of time. Finally we reach our stop and I get off, along with Ethan and some other kids. My brother and I clomp through the snow toward our house. The streets are barely plowed, and icy pellets are pinging my face. Unpleasant. Aggravating. Just, ugh.

"Isn't this awesome!" Ethan grins, kicking piles of snow as we walk. His jacket's not even zipped.

Now it's me who grunts, like he did this morning. "I'd rather be at school."

"You're crazy!" Ethan shouts, then clomp-runs the rest of the way home.

Maybe. But he's crazier.

CHAPTER TWO

Thrown Together

ETHAN

I plod up the driveway to the garage—one snowdrift is almost to my knees—then punch the code on the number pad. The garage opens and a heap of snow blows inside. I'm digging in my backpack for my key, but Erin brushes past me with her key already out.

Once we're in the laundry room, Erin takes off her jacket and arranges it neatly over the sink. I fling mine on top of the washing machine, but it slides to the floor. She does the eye-roll/head-shake *I can't believe you* look. I do the *what's the big deal* shrug. As we do with most things.

We walk into the kitchen and I pull open the pantry door. Not much in the way of snacks, like usual. Erin unzips her backpack and takes out a folder. "I suppose I can work ahead in LA."

"And do what?" I ask. "We didn't even have LA today."

"Oh, I'll think of something."

"Here's an idea! With this extra bonus time, why not finish the report for Mrs. D'Antonio?"

She puts a hand on her hip. "I told you, there's still more research to go over."

"How much more is there, Rin? Kids' brains work better when they can move around. We need a standing-desk option in school. End of story."

She goes, "I wish it were that simple."

"But it *is* that simple! Come *on*. My butt can't survive much longer."

"Well, your butt will just have to be patient."

"It's been patient! Now it's losing hope!" I careen into the family room and fall onto the sofa face-first.

She comes into the room; I see her white socks from the corner of my eye. "Ethan. Do you want to convince Mrs. D'Antonio or not?"

I moan into the cushions. "I do."

"I'm close to being done. A few more days. A week, tops."

I roll over. "A week! We need to get moving on this, and fast. *Moving*, get it?"

"Yes, very funny." She gets her backpack. "Fine. I'll work on it now."

"Thank you!"

She goes upstairs and shuts her door.

This all started about two months ago, when I kind of snapped in LA from scoma overload, stood up, and said I was "protesting" how long we have to sit at our desks. I've always had a thing with sitting. No ADHD, but something Dad jokingly calls ESD. Ethan Squiggle Disease.

Anyway, my LA teacher, Mr. Delman, told me to sit down . . . and I didn't. I got sent to Mrs. D'Antonio's office; then I told her *she* should sit all day and see how it feels. She didn't appreciate that statement. I ended up with two after-school sessions of Reflection—McNutt's nice word for detention.

Ms. Gilardi, the eighth-grade science teacher who supervises Reflection, urged me to channel my energy into Invention Day. That's always been Erin's deal, not mine, but I came up with the desk-evator idea so people could stand if/when needed. I recruited Brian, and we made what I thought was a good-enough prototype with basic kitchen materials. It got the point across, but the people at Invention Day were pros. We were so out of our league. They had robotics, and solar panels, and *swag*!

Enter my sister. The week after Invention Day, Erin stood up for me (literally) and got everyone to do a real protest during LA—she cleverly called it a stand-in. Delman said he'd consider the standing-desk idea. That is, *after* we put together a detailed report for D'Antonio, making our case.

And here we are. Butt solidly in chair, no report. Erin's better at that kind of stuff than me, so I agreed she should put it together. But the way she goes about researching a topic, this could take until spring.

I roll off the sofa, crawl up the stairs, then knock on her door. "Can I please see what you have so far?"

She flings open the door. "Oh, all right! But only if you stop badgering me!" She sits at her desk. "Just know this is not where it needs to be."

I stand next to her as she flips through several PowerPoint slides on her laptop, explaining each one. When she gets to the last slide, I go, "How can this not be done? You have everything."

"Are you kidding me? This is thrown together."

"Thrown together? Erin! It's the best presentation I've ever seen! If this won't convince Mrs. D'Antonio, I don't know what will."

"Thank you, but I think it needs a few more visuals. A couple more statistics. Maybe video."

"No, it's great! Let's ask if we can show it to her tomorrow!"

"It's not ready." She pulls up a website. "I haven't read this research yet. There might be some relevant information."

"It doesn't have to be perfect!" I shout.

"Um, yes, it does."

I stamp my foot. "Why do you have to make everything such a major production?"

Erin narrows her eyes. "I resent that comment when I am helping you."

"Sorry. I say we go with this."

"And I say we don't."

We glare at each other for a few seconds. Our little stand-in is turning into a big standoff. A place I know all too well when it comes to my sister.

Erin's phone buzzes and she picks it up. "Dad wants you to go out and shovel."

I groan loudly, then barrel down the stairs. Boots, jacket, gloves, hat—on. I bang my fist on the garage-door opener, grab a shovel, and wade onto the driveway. "And I say we don't," I mutter, imitating Erin's voice.

It's still coming down, and it's the wet, heavy kind of snow. I start a path, then turn around and see Erin— her room faces the street and her desk is by the window. She's looking down with her usual intense face. Why is everything a *thing* with her? Why can't she ever do something without index cards and a hundred hours of preparation? I bet she would've finished the report a lot sooner if *she* were getting continual scomas.

I jam the shovel into a large drift, then turn into a shoveling maniac, attacking pile after pile. It takes me I don't know how long, but finally the driveway's clear except for one monster snow boulder by the mailbox that I'm sure was left by the plow.

I hear Erin's voice from the garage. "Ethan! Come in already! You're going to get frostbite!"

I shake my head and she runs back inside. I'm finishing this. I try to chip away at the edges of the boulder. Not working. It's more ice than snow. I drop the shovel and then, with all my strength, roll it into our side yard. I leave it right in front of the two Adirondack chairs that everyone likes to sit in on summer days. Everyone except me.

I have this sinking feeling that scomas are gonna be a part of my life for a long, long time.

ERIN

When Mom gets home, she's full of stories about how long it took her and how many cars skidded off the road and how the plows can't keep up. She walks wearily to the stairs. "Ethan?"

Some sort of inaudible reply comes from my brother's room.

"Thanks for doing the driveway!" She drops onto the sofa and puts her feet up on the table. "I'm so glad you've both been home safe this whole time. What've you been doing?"

"Ethan shoveled. I worked on the report. He thinks it's ready, but believe me, it's not. It's *far* from ready."

Mom's phone rings. "Can you grab it, hon? That car ride was exhausting."

I get the phone from her purse, run it back to her. She taps the call, listens, then hangs up. "Automated message from McNutt. Snow day tomorrow, guys."

Ethan races down the stairs. "Really?" He jumps and shoots an invisible ball. "Frankenstorm, I love you! You just keep making my day."

Dad comes in, also talking about the traffic and weather and stuck cars. "It's a real mess out there."

Ethan interrupts. "What about dinner? I'm starving."

"We'll have to improvise," Mom says. "I was planning to stop at the store, but then I just wanted to get home."

Dad opens the freezer and holds up a package of egg rolls. "Jackpot!" Mom finds a family-size box of mac 'n' cheese in the pantry that's just past the expiration date. She laughs. "I don't think it'll kill us." They add in a couple of other random items: applesauce, and chips and salsa. Interesting meal.

When we sit down, Ethan rips a bite from an egg roll like he hasn't eaten in days. "Did you finish the report?" he asks me.

"Not yet."

"C'mon, you were working on it the whole time I shoveled, right?"

"Pretty much."

"So . . ."

"Well, there's still—"

Ethan slaps the table with his palm and turns to Mom and Dad. "The report is done. It's great, I swear! If I were Mrs. D and I watched it, I'd get standing desks in school so fast, everyone's head would spin. And my ESD would be history!"

Mom glances at me. "Thoughts?"

"I want to go over it again. It has to be superb."

"It's already superb!" Ethan exclaims.

"Listen to your sister's opinion," Dad says. "Consider her feelings."

"Thank you," I say.

Ethan does this long, overly dramatic sigh. "Mom. Dad. Feel free to ditch your parenting philosophies and step in anytime to tell Erin she overthinks things—"

I huff. "I do *not* overthink things!"

Dad clears his throat.

"I mean, not all the time. Not with everything."

Mom dips a chip in the salsa. "You know we don't operate like that, Ethan. You two need to solve this on your own."

Dad nods. "Put your heads together after dinner and come up with a compromise," he says.

Ethan groans. "The compromise will be that Erin won't say it's finished until Erin says it's finished."

"If that's what it is, then that's what it is." I help myself to some mac 'n' cheese and raise an eyebrow at Ethan. "You need me, you know."

"Yeah, that's the problem."

"You're welcome to do it by yourself. I'll delete the whole thing and you can start over."

"No, don't do that!" He slumps in his chair. "Fine! I'll wait!"

"Good choice. It'll be worth it." I stab some noodles with my fork. "I promise."

"Okay," he grumbles.

I chew the noodles five times, then swallow. What? I like to do things the way I think they should be done, okay?

CHAPTER THREE

Snow Day

ETHAN

When I wake up, the snow has stopped. Dad and I clear the driveway again. Then, weirdly, by noon the sun is shining.

I'd just like to mention that Erin didn't pick up a shovel once during Frankenstorm. But I'm letting her have a bye because I'm praying she finished the report. No word yet. Her door's been shut all morning.

Also all morning, Zoe's been texting me.

Are you doing anything? Let's hang out! Wanna go sledding? We should make a snow person! It's beautiful outside!!! Doesn't it look like Narnia? I love it!!!

An overload of exclamation points, plus hearts and snowflakes after "love." I have no idea what to do about this thing with Zoe. Wait, I don't mean it's a *thing*! I mean it's out of control. Out of *my* control.

I sort of like her, but I'm not sure if I *like* like her or want to have a *girlfriend*. Because then you have to buy her cute little presents like stuffed animals and candy, and go to the mall and movies. Isn't that how it works? Brian's dying to have a girlfriend. Why doesn't Zoe like *him*?

Speaking of, Brian texts me and begs to come over. My mom wants me to help her cook kielbasa. U know how that looks? And smells? Escape route needed ASAP.

He lives on the block behind ours, so he gets here pretty fast. We go downstairs to the basement and play this game we made up with a ball and Dad's broken air hockey table he had when he was a kid. Why he saved it, I don't know. It's never worked.

Brian stands behind the line and tosses the ball toward the table. "You gotta gimme your take on the Veronica Lee situation, okay? I talk to her every day in math, right? I crack jokes about how Mrs. Genovese is so old she has a pet dinosaur and lives in a cave. Veronica always laughs. I gave her this little rainbow eraser I found in the gym. She uses it every day!"

"Sounds promising." I take my shot; the ball bounces off the table and hits a wall.

"I sing 'Veronica' to her all the time."

"There's a song called 'Veronica'?"

"Yeah. Elvis Costello sings it."

I elbow him. "I'd go out with you."

"Great. I don't want to date *you*. My question is, how come I can't get past school-friend status? I'm taller. I've grown an inch! I'm funny. Aren't I funny? Tell me I'm funny."

"You're funny." I get the ball, try to twirl it on my fingertip. "Maybe you should, like, not be so all over her."

He stares at me. "What are you talking about? Then she'd never even notice me."

The basement door opens and I hear my sister's and Zoe's voices. A minute later the two of them come down the stairs.

"Hi, Ethan!" Zoe waves.

"Hi."

She skips over, then hugs me. I don't know what to do, so I sort of end up patting her ponytail.

She steps back. "It's amazing out there, you guys! The

snow is like magic crystals! You almost don't want to walk on it, you know? But we should. We should get out there and experience it. Breathe it in."

"We're in the middle of something important here," Brian says.

"What?" Erin asks, glancing around.

"Nothing you need to know about."

Erin rolls her eyes. "Oh, okay." She motions to Zoe. "Come on, let's go upstairs. There's nothing to do down here."

"We can just hang out." Zoe plops onto the sofa.

Brian's looking at his phone. "News flash. Veronica's at the toboggan hill with Sky Jeon and some other people. She posted a picture. Do you think she likes him? She probably likes him. It looks like she likes him." He enlarges the picture with his thumb and finger. "It's impossible to compete with that kind of coolness."

"She likes him," Erin says bluntly.

"For sure?" Brian asks. I swear, he looks like he might cry.

Erin shrugs. "I thought you knew. Everyone else does."

"Not true," I interrupt. "I heard Mason likes Sky."

Erin shakes her head. "Mason doesn't like Sky. He likes

Jack. Why don't you guys ever know what's going on?"

I cross my arms. "We know things. That are going on."

"Okay," Erin says. "Sure."

Zoe bolts up. "I have an idea! Let's walk to Starbucks! Doesn't a steaming cup of hot chocolate sound great right now?"

Brian's still staring at his phone. "This image is now burned into my mind forever."

"Bri." I pull the phone from his hands. "Maybe we should go. You need some air."

He nods sadly. Then we all file upstairs, put on our gear, and go outside. Zoe circles her arms as I close the garage. "See? Look around, you guys! Isn't it beautiful?" She comes up next to me. "What kind of hot chocolate do you like?"

"I don't know—how many kinds are there?"

"Oh, they have regular, peppermint, salted caramel, molten, snickerdoodle, tuxedo . . ."

"Regular's fine, I guess."

"Really? Me too! We like the same kind!"

As we start walking, she links her arm through mine. Brian raises his eyebrows and shoots me a grin, and I just, I don't know, I just walk.

ZOE

Can we talk about Ethan for a second? If this is even possible, he's gotten cuter in the last few weeks. Maybe someone gets cuter when you realize how much you like him? I'll have to see if there's an online quiz about that.

We went to a movie a few weeks ago. I chose one carefully—not a potentially embarrassing rom-com, nothing bloody or violent. But not a kid movie either. It was based on a book we read last year in LA. Perfect.

He bought the tickets, so for sure it qualified as an actual date! I was waiting for him to hold my hand or put his arm around me, but he didn't. His awkward shyness just made me melt even more. I was almost going to kiss him again before I got out of the car, but it felt too weird with his dad in the front seat.

When we text, his answers are always short and sweet, like "hey," and "okay," and "see ya." How adorable is that?

Don't worry! I assure you I haven't forgotten about the imminent peril facing our planet. I will return to the Be Green Club when my heart has settled down. Although . . . it might be a while.

It looks like everything is covered with a giant white blanket—snow on every rooftop and tree, sparkling in the sun. Chimneys with their little puffs of smoke coming out, the cloudless blue sky. It doesn't even look real. More like a painting.

I unhook my arm from Ethan's and breathe it all in. "Most people don't know that snow is environmentally necessary."

No one replies. Ethan and Brian knock into each other, then laugh, and Erin's bundled up, only her eyes peeking out.

"It insulates and protects plant life from freezing temperatures and damaging winds. And when it melts, snow provides moisture to plants during the winter months. It replenishes the water supply too. Isn't that interesting, how nature has a purpose for everything?"

"Very," Brian says.

"Don't make fun of her," Erin says. "It *is* interesting, Zoe."

Brian kicks some snow in Erin's direction.

"Hey," she scoffs. "It's not my fault if Veronica likes someone else."

"Thanks for bringing that up again," Brian mutters.

"Yeah," Ethan adds. "Really, Erin. You had to say that?"

"Just telling it like it is," she says, then walks ahead a little.

We turn the corner and I see Starbucks in the distance. Brian makes a snowball and tosses it toward Erin's back. It just misses her. She whips around, picks up a handful of snow, and throws it at him. He dodges it, grinning, his arms in the air.

I fall in step with Ethan. "You know, they're actually kind of cute together."

"Uh . . . I don't think so."

"They are! Opposites attract and all that. They have a definite chemistry." I listen to everyone's boots crunch in unison. "This is so fun, you guys! We're, like, a group now, the four of us."

Brian turns around. "We're not a group. Maybe you think we're a group, but I don't think we're a group. We're just four people walking."

I smile to myself. We're a group.

We pass a line of snow people in front of a house. "Don't those heads look really small?" Ethan says.

Brian nods. "Uh-huh. It's a disease. Shrunken snow-ball heads."

Erin looks at him. "What?"

"Forget it. Just making a joke."

"Oh, that's what that was?"

He glares at her.

We cross the street and reach Starbucks. Brian runs to the door, holds it open, bows, and makes a sweeping gesture with his arm. "After you, Erin McBarren."

"Why is everything in my life so dysfunctional?" Erin says, then goes inside.

Brian follows her. "Maybe you're the one who's dysfunctional."

"See what I mean?" I whisper to Ethan. "Really kind of cute."

BRIAN

I spot her right away: Veronica, with the undeniable cool-ness of Sky Jeon next to her. The two of them look cozy, sitting at a table in the back with some other people.

I turn around, bumping into Zoe. "We have to go," I say. "Right now."

"Why? We just got here." She glances around. "Seems like a lot of people from school had the same idea."

"Yeah." I tip my head toward the back. Ethan and Zoe look over. Then I hear Veronica laugh. Her cute, crinkly-eyed, shoulder-shaking laugh. Great, just great. I'll sit here the whole time, watching her with Sky out of the corner of my eye, listening to that laugh. First, I was obsessed with Jamie Pappas, but she liked Armando. Now Veronica goes for Sky. I'm 0 for 2.

Ethan says, "If you bolt out of here, that's kind of . . ."

"Kind of what? Lame? Weak?"

Zoe puts a hand on my arm. "Let's just get our hot chocolate and sit by the window, okay? C'mon, Erin's already in line. It'll be fine."

"I think she saw you," Ethan says, glancing over my shoulder as we're paying. "She's looking over here."

I don't turn around. I grab my hot chocolate—I don't even know what I ordered—and hightail it to the farthest-away table I can find. Ethan, Erin, and Zoe pull up chairs. I hear that laugh again as Veronica and Sky and the others walk through the place, finally going out the door. I want to pull off that little jingly bell and stomp on it until it jingles no more.

Zoe says, "Okay, she's gone. You can relax now. Drink your hot chocolate."

I take a sip and burn the roof of my mouth immediately. Ah, who am I kidding? I'm one inch taller. So what! I'm still one of the shortest guys in seventh grade. I haven't started shaving because there's nothing to shave, unless I want to shave the new crop of pimples on my face. And let's not even talk about how I can't find a deodorant that works. Everyone uses Axe, but it gives me a rash. What do you even do about that? And who do you even ask!

That stupid bell jingles again. If it's Jamie with Armando, I swear . . .

"Oh no," Erin says, pulling her hat lower and sliding down in her chair. "This is apparently the day to see everyone you don't want to see."

Just then, Marlon Romanov walks in.

ERIN

He's by himself. Just as I would expect.

"And the plot thickens," Brian says in a teasing voice,

pretending to hold a microphone. "Enter McNutt's mystery man. Scary tech genius, dressed in black, Erin Marcus's archenemy. Cue the ominous music. Dum-dum-dum-dummm."

I don't even bother to respond to Brian's nonsense. Marlon goes over to the register with his typical smug, arrogant expression. He's wearing black jeans and a black jacket, as per usual. Like he's too cool for a striped shirt or regular blue jeans. He's probably ordering espresso or cappuccino.

"Look, Erin has steam coming out of her nose," Brian says.

I raise an eyebrow. "Not funny."

Ethan jabs Brian, then goes, "Erin, I know you have an issue with him, but try to chill, okay?"

"I *am* chill! I am very chill. *Super-extremely* chill."

Ethan says, "Right, uh-huh."

Marlon pays, then stands at the counter to wait for his drink, staring straight ahead. He never smiles or looks angry or sad or anything. He's like . . . emotionless.

At Invention Day last year in sixth grade, Marlon won. He told me—are you ready for this—that men are better than girls at science. Girls! He didn't even say *women*. I was so stunned, I just stood there. I thought of several perfect, sarcastic responses later on, believe me, but in the moment I was struck silent.

This year I was hoping with all my heart to beat him, but it didn't happen. Due to a series of mishaps—mostly involving a football, Brian, and my brother—Zoe's and my invention to stop the spread of invasive plants didn't work as we envisioned. We did, however, get a special honorable mention, and we're determined to return next year with success.

At least Marlon didn't win. He was disqualified because he didn't make the required trifold display board. I'm sure he thought he was above that. Parneeta won with her parachute-fabric backpack invention, which I'll admit I was surprised took first. I realize it was extremely lightweight, durable, and cool-looking, but a *backpack*?

Anyway, after the awards were announced, I marched up to Marlon, making sure he was aware that *women* took first, second, and third place. But you know what he did? He stalked out of the gym without a word. No reply whatsoever!

Actually, there might be steam coming out of my nose.

I sip my hot chocolate, dribbling some on my chin. "Erin," Zoe says, handing me a napkin, "just ignore him. As I told you at Invention Day, he's not worth it. Don't waste your energy on him."

I close my eyes and take a deep, long breath as Zoe would undoubtedly advise. And three breaths later, forget it. I'm sweating profusely and can feel my hair frizzing. I peel off my hat and pull my hair into a bun on top of my head. Why do they keep it so warm in here? It has to be eighty degrees!

Marlon gets his drink and walks out without a glance at anyone. Who does he think he is? So full of himself, like he knows everything and he's better than everyone.

Zoe, Ethan, and Brian are talking about a video with a dog doing flips on a trampoline or something. I don't know—I'm barely listening. I crane my neck and see Marlon get into a sleek silver car. It drives off, leaving a long trail of whitish smoke. Ugh, ugh, ugh. There are just some people in this world you wish you never crossed paths with.

CHAPTER FOUR

The Invites

ETHAN

Wednesday we're back at school and the fun is over. Butt in chair in math, no report from Erin. Another day of scomas in a long line of never-ending scomas.

Before the first-period bell rings, Mrs. Genovese shuffles toward my desk. She gives me this teacher *look* and I immediately realize what it's about. I forgot to SHARPEN THE PENCIL I borrowed on Monday.

"Ethan?" she says, lowering her enormous round glasses and gazing down at me.

"Uh . . . yeah?"

"I have something for you."

That's it. She's sending me to pencil jail.

Instead she hands me a hall pass. "You're supposed to go see Ms. Gilardi."

I stare at the pass. So, this isn't about the pencil?

"Ms. Gilardi? Now?" I ask.

"Yes. She wanted to see you first thing, so it must be pretty important."

I grab my stuff and leave with everyone looking at me. Things rarely turn out well when a teacher pulls you out of a class.

When I get to Gilardi's room, I see Romanov sitting at a desk in the back. Brian's leaning on the counter by the window, and Erin and Zoe are there too, sitting in the first row. No one's talking. What the heck is going on?

Gilardi motions to me. "Ethan, come in." She's got a long scarf looped around her neck, and I wonder if that's what she was knitting when I was in here for Reflection. Are we all in trouble? What did I do?

"Take a seat," she says. "Or stand, if you prefer. That's perfectly fine with me." I go over to Brian. "You know what this is about?" I whisper.

"Not a clue. Can't be good."

Gilardi doesn't look mad, though. In fact she's, like, beaming at us. "Okay, great, we're all here. I'm so glad I have a free period right now, because I have some exciting news to share. And let me tell you, it's been extraordinarily difficult to keep this under wraps for the last few weeks. But I didn't want to say anything until I knew for sure."

We're all glancing at each other for any kind of hint, but everyone looks confused. Everyone except Romanov. He looks the same as always—like this is incredibly boring and he'd rather be somewhere else.

"Have any of you heard of Zak Canzeri? Better known to the world as Z?" Gilardi asks.

Erin raises her hand. "I've heard of him. I follow him on social media."

"Excellent! Do you know what he does?"

Erin nods. Of course she knows.

"He created a couple of popular apps and built a start-up a few years ago. Something with an online payment system, if I remember correctly."

"That's right!" Ms. Gilardi exclaims. "Z is quite the success. One of those twentysomething Silicon Valley wonders."

Brian crosses one foot over the other. "What does that have to do with us?"

Gilardi points at him. "Glad you asked. Not only is Z a young sensation, but he's very generous with his time. Z is committed to growing the future generation of techpreneurs. A term he coined himself."

Erin leans forward and her eyes get wide. "Are you talking about his innovation camps?"

Gilardi clasps her hands. "Yes!"

"His what camps?" Brian says.

"Z runs exclusive pop-up tech camps for kids," Gilardi says. "Zak Canzeri Innovation Camp, or as they call them, ZCIC. No one knows when the next one will be. They're very secretive about the process." She looks at each of us, slowly, one by one. "I can now reveal that I nominated all of you for the next ZCIC when I learned it was going to be held in northern Illinois."

My sister gasps, but all I'm thinking is, *I'm not in trouble. . . . I've been* nominated *for something.*

Brian stabs a finger at his chest. "Wait, me?"

In a hushed voice Zoe says, "I'm so honored."

And Marlon is silent.

"I think it's best if you hear the next part from Z himself." Gilardi opens her laptop and taps the keys. "Gather 'round, everyone."

We stand near the laptop. Erin claps a hand across

her heart as a shiny gold *Z* comes on the screen, surrounded by lightning bolts. Classical music plays. Then the *Z* and the lightning bolts fade away, the music stops, and this guy appears. He's wearing dark sunglasses, a black jacket, and black pants, and he looks really tall—at least six-five, I'd guess. "Hello, friends," he says. "I am Zak Canzeri. But please, call me Z, as the world does. It is my distinct pleasure to inform you that you have been invited to attend the next ZCIC. Our exclusive coterie, if you will."

"Coterie?" I repeat.

Erin whips her head around. "Shh! It's a small group of people with shared interests." She quickly turns back to the screen. How does Erin know words that no one else knows? Except Zak Canzeri, obviously.

Z continues. "ZCIC is an invention, maker, business, and tech camp all in one. Only one hundred young people are invited to each session. Simply put, it is a life-changing experience. You will invent, design, build, and showcase. You will create a real or virtual entity and put together a complete business plan. On the final day, you will present your work to a panel of experts and potential investors. Congratulations. We hope to see you there."

He smiles with his mouth closed; then the screen goes to black. The gold *Z* returns, pops and sizzles like a firecracker, then disappears. He never took off the sunglasses the whole time he was talking. Kinda weird, but maybe that's standard for Silicon Valley sensations?

Erin's face is shiny and she's panting a little. "I—I don't know what to say! I'm in shock, absolute shock! This is amazing! I've seen posts that some of the kids' inventions from ZCIC have become actual products."

"That's true, Erin." Gilardi closes the laptop. We all stand around her, but Romanov goes to the desk he was sitting at in the back of the room.

"The most wonderful part of ZCIC," Gilardi explains, "is that the sky's the limit. Invent an app or a drone or a robot. Focus on the environment, a health issue, or even something fun. Anything and everything."

"When is the camp?" Zoe asks.

"Oh! Of course, the details." Gilardi picks up some papers from her desk and hands one to each of us. "It's during the second week of winter break. I sincerely hope that all of you can take part in this one-of-a-kind experience. I know it's rather short notice, but that's how they do it. People drop everything to be at one of these."

Erin's holding the paper with trembling hands. "A printed invitation on white stationery. With gold lettering."

I look down at mine. There's my name, typed and, yes, in gold. It even says "Mr.," as in Mr. Ethan Marcus. Okay, I get Erin and Zoe being nominated, and of course Romanov. No question there. But . . . *me and Brian*?

He must be thinking the same thing. "Uh . . . ," he says. "You're sure you meant to nominate me?"

Gilardi laughs. "I'll be honest, I considered several students, and it wasn't an easy choice. I could only nominate five. I was looking for a quality that's hard to pin down but you know it when you see it. An inner passion, I suppose. Not simply making something by following a plan, but embracing the true spirit of invention. Being creative and curious. Pushing the boundaries without even realizing you're doing it."

I have all *that*? She got that from seeing my *desk-evator*?

Zoe blinks, like she's trying not to cry. "I can't thank you enough for this opportunity."

Gilardi nods. "I know, it's overwhelming."

Marlon still hasn't said a word.

Gilardi unloops her scarf and drapes it over her chair. "The ZCIC motto is TADA. It stands for Tenacity, Appetite, Determination, Aim."

Brian smirks. "I always knew I was a TADA kinda guy."

Gilardi looks back at Marlon. "The robotic hand." She gestures to Erin and Zoe. "The All-Natural Invasive Plant Destroyer." Finally she turns to me and Brian. "The deskalator."

"Desk-evator," I say. Although that would've been a good name. I didn't think of that.

"Right. What I saw at Invention Day from you five, well, that was TADA."

Erin turns her head slowly, then gapes at me. Well, whaddya know? For once in our lives, my sister and I are on the same level.

CHAPTER FIVE

The Reactions

ERIN

Ms. Gilardi goes over details about registering for the camp and urges us to talk to our parents ASAP. No worries there. First thing on tonight's agenda.

Zoe and I walk out together. I'm still in shock. "Zak Canzeri Innovation Camp! Can you believe this in a million years?"

"I know. It's incredible."

Everything in the hall is a blur. My cerebrum is absolutely buzzing. I'll need to have an idea in mind before I arrive on the first day. A fully fleshed-out concept, perhaps. Maybe even an outline of my business plan too. I'm going to be competing with the best of the best.

Which is why I'm having trouble wrapping my head

around Ms. Gilardi's choice of my brother and Brian. The spirit of invention, creativity—a bit of a stretch, but okay. Except for one crucial fact. They made the desk-evator out of spatulas, chip clips, and a broken cutting board. They used *duct tape*!

I can tell you right now, even though I've never been to a ZCIC, I know that kind of sloppiness won't cut it.

I turn toward Zoe. "From what I've seen online, these camps are super intense. You have to . . ." Her bottom lip is quivering, and it looks like she might burst into tears any second. "What's wrong?"

She sniffles. "The camp is the same time that I'm supposed to go visit my relatives in Michigan. We're staying a few days. My aunt and uncle and cousins."

"Well, there's no discussion here. You simply have to get out of it. Once your mom understands that this is a once-in-a-lifetime opportunity, she won't make you go. There's no way! You can stay at my house."

Zoe's face brightens. "Okay! You're right. I'll talk to her." She ducks into her classroom.

Before I go into science, I quickly read over the first

paragraph of the invitation again, making 100 percent sure I didn't imagine the events of the last half hour.

> Dear Ms. Erin Marcus,
> You are cordially invited to attend a five-day
> session of the prestigious, highly selective
> Zak Canzeri Innovation Camp (ZCIC), to
> be held on the campus of Colton College
> in Forest Hill, Illinois, from December 26
> to 30. Congratulations! You are part of an
> elite group of one hundred carefully chosen
> students. Z looks forward to welcoming you.

Did you hear that? It's real. Z looks forward to welcoming *me*! I've seen tweets and videos about the camps, but never thought that *I* would be invited to one.

This. This changes *everything*.

ZOE

When I get home after school, no one's around. Mom's at work, and my little sister, Hannah, is at a friend's house. I'm secretly glad. Hannah and I share a room, and she chatters nonstop about everything that comes into her mind. There are times I need quiet and privacy. You know.

I have to make Mom understand about the camp. She doesn't exactly get things like this. Dad would've, but he's not here. I suppose I could try to text him, but he's in Thailand. It's, what, like four a.m. there? And anyway, what difference would it make if I reached him?

I go into my room, sit on the edge of my bed, and hug my sunflower pillow. I always try to be positive, because negative thoughts never help a situation, but I admit I've been dreading the Michigan trip. Let's just say that side of the family is not exactly my cup of organic chamomile tea.

Aunt Marci is Mom's older sister, and she's sort of Erin-ish. Always telling Mom what to do and not to do. With Erin, I can hold my own when I need to. And I know that deep down Erin has a good, well-meaning heart. It might not seem like it sometimes, but she does. Like when Dad didn't come back from Thailand after he met Dara, Erin was there for me. She'd split her cookie with me at lunch or come to the Be Green Club meetings when no one else did.

But Mom never holds her own with her sister. And I'm not so sure about the quality of Aunt Marci's heart.

I press my lips together and hold back a sob. Mom can't make me go, not now! Besides, Ethan was invited to the camp too! Maybe we can work on a project together if they allow that.

I know, you're probably thinking I'm too into him. The truth is, I like Ethan *a lot*, but there's more to it. I want to, *need* to, believe in love with all my brainpower. Because really, when it comes down to it, if you don't believe in love, how can you believe in anything in the universe?

My parents have been divorced since I was nine (Hannah was only six), but it was okay. That's not what I'm talking about. Mom and Dad got along better, and Dad and I had our Saturdays. We'd go to the nature center, take long hikes, and discuss how to save the planet. He's the one who got me interested in environmental issues in the first place.

But a year ago Dad went on a business trip to Thailand, got an eye infection while he was there, and fell in love with the doctor who treated him. (That would be Dara.) He told us he wasn't coming back. Mom hung up on him, and that's been it. Dad and I texted at first, but now not so much.

Aunt Marci calls all the time to tell Mom how she never actually liked Dad and how terrible it is that he abandoned me and Hannah. Her voice is loud. I hear everything.

And let me add this: Aunt Marci does not believe in recycling. She says it doesn't make a difference. They throw everything away. When we visit, she uses paper plates and Styrofoam cups! It's so upsetting. Can you imagine how much garbage they must produce? I can't bear to think about it.

How can I convince Mom to let me go to the camp instead of to Michigan? She doesn't see Marci the way I do, so I can't bring her into this. I grab a piece of note-book paper from my backpack and find my favorite pen, made from recycled plastic water bottles. I need at least five solid, strong, surefire reasons that have nothing to do with my aunt.

BRIAN

My brother, John, picks up the invitation when he comes in. I left it on the kitchen table with my pile of homework.

Hard to miss that giant gold *Z* jumping off the paper.

He does a laugh-smirk after he reads it. "You got invited to one of these? Man, they must really be lowering their standards."

"Hey!" I grab the paper from him. "This teacher nominated me and Ethan, okay! Because of what we did at Invention Day. She thinks we have, uh . . ." I can't remember what TADA stands for. "Talent!"

"Seriously?"

"Yeah, seriously."

John shakes his head. "Brian, the people who go to these camps get jobs at, like, Google and Apple. They're supposed to be pretty insane. I know this guy who knows someone in New Jersey who went to one, and he was so freaked out, he didn't go back after the first day. He had to take meds to calm down, apparently. They massacred him."

"*Massacred?* Come on, that story can't be true."

He shrugs as he pulls his phone from his pocket. "Just tellin' you what I heard."

My brother's in high school. Maybe it's true. He knows things I know nothing about.

So the first thing I think is that someone in Zak Canzeri's office is going to be fired. It's one thing for Gilardi to be blind and nominate us because she thinks we have inner passion and TADA and all that, but it's another thing for them to actually believe her and *invite* us.

Second thing I think: It's got to be a mess-up. Some kind of computer error. The wrong name or something. I'm willing to put money on the fact that there's another Brian Kowalski somewhere in Illinois who was supposed to get this invitation.

Then, bam, it hits me. Third thing. What if this is a setup? They purposely invite idiots like me and Ethan just so we can freak out like that guy in New Jersey and not come back. It's their secret plan, to scare people, show them how serious this is so they don't fool around. We could be the slacker examples! That's it. That has to be it. Number three wins.

I grab my phone, text Ethan, tell him my theory.

I don't know, he says. I guess it's possible.

What r u gonna do? I reply. Are u going?

Are u?

I asked u first.

He sends me a bunch of question marks.

I type a bunch of exclamation points.

Then he sends me a photo of a spatula.

From the DE? Good times, I reply. Glad that's over.

The truth is, I never wanted to do Invention Day. I only agreed because I thought it would impress Jamie, and we know how that turned out. I told her my feelings at ID and she friend-zoned me in front of several hundred people. Not my best moment.

What if we went to the camp and took another crack at the desk-evator? Ethan says. Did a business plan, a whole strategy, all that stuff Gilardi was talking about.

I stare at my screen. What's he saying? I don't even know how to respond. Because it's the most ludicrous idea I've ever heard. And besides, how do you tell your best friend he's lost his freakin' mind over this desk-evator thing?

You tell him, okay? Someone has to.

ETHAN

Brian isn't answering. I'm gonna go out on a limb and take a guess he doesn't want to go to the camp. The only way I got him to do Invention Day was by telling him that

Jamie liked smart guys. I kinda had heard someone say that; wasn't sure if it was really true.

Anyway, doesn't matter: We blew it. No doubt about that. I admit it, I didn't have a clue. But now *this*. Something really good came out of my mess-up.

I remember my measly little desk-evator, standing unsteadily by itself on our table, without balloons or streamers or swag, and how I felt like an idiot compared to everyone else in the gym that night. But now I see it differently, like it was on a dark stage under a single glowing spotlight. Like maybe my creation didn't look as bad as I felt like it did.

Gilardi said I have what she was looking for. Can you believe it? She thought I was embracing the true spirit of invention! And I have tenacity . . . and that other stuff.

I'm not even sure what tenacity is, exactly, but I should know if I have it, right? When I look up the word, I find out it means persistence. Determination. Resolve.

Okay. I'm good with that. That's some cool stuff to have.

There's only one question, then.

What if Brian's right? What if it's all a setup?

M.R.

My parents insist that I go to a regular school, take regular classes. They want me to grow up "normal." Not be treated "special." Make friends. Join a club or play a sport. Go to a basketball game. They assure me these endeavors will be fun and will "help."

What my parents do not understand is that when you are like me, normal is (1) not easy or (2) not something I can simply decide to be.

It is more like attempting to navigate a labyrinth where the other participants have been given a map but I am on my own in a strange, confusing land.

They also do not understand how difficult it is to be in that land.

These are some of the reasons why being home is preferable to being at school. There are no mazes or maps. No club meetings where I stand with my hand on the doorknob for 87.5 seconds and listen to the kids but never go inside the room.

It is not difficult to be home, even though none of the houses or apartments have felt particularly warm or comfortable. We haven't been in any of them very long.

Mom always says, "Dad's company is our home." We leave when they promote him and tell him to go to another city for a more important position. He moves "up the ladder" and we move with him.

The first house, I remember, had ivy on the fence and jade-green shutters on the windows. I taught myself to read when we lived there. I was three years and two months old. There was a swing set in the back from the family that had lived there before, but I wasn't interested. Mom found that unusual. I suppose that was the beginning.

She worried why I never wanted to play on it. It had a yellow flag and THE HIDEOUT carved into the wood. When the weather was amenable, Mom would say, "Let's go swing, Marlon," but I shook my head. I was immersed in a challenge of some sort. A puzzle, dominoes, the Rubik's Cube.

I never swung. Not once.

The day before we left that house, I found a screwdriver in one of the boxes and tightened the bolts for the next family. I was five years and six months old. Perhaps one of their children would want to use the swing set,

I thought. Dad asked me how I learned to use a screwdriver. He was baffled. I didn't have an answer; I just knew how.

My parents do not realize it, but many times they add to the difficulty.

I must attend the Zak Canzeri Innovation Camp. I have been waiting all my life for this.

CHAPTER SIX

Treasure Hunt

ETHAN

For the last hour, Erin's been pacing around the family room, shuffling index cards and talking to herself. "What're you doing?" I finally ask.

"Don't say anything to Mom and Dad about the invitation, okay? I have a little surprise planned for when they get home. A very cool way to tell them the incredible news."

"What is it?"

"A treasure hunt! With clues that I'm going to hide around the house!"

"Can't you just tell them?"

"No! This is big, Ethan. It's really big. I've been looking on the ZCIC website. Z is a big thinker. He comes up with big things."

"So, lemme get this straight—you're saying this is big?"

"Stop! Don't do that. Not now. Not with this."

"Am I included in your treasure hunt? I got invited too, in case you forgot."

"Um, no. You can announce it to Mom and Dad yourself, in your own way." She gives me a sort of pity smile. "It was nice of Ms. Gilardi to nominate you."

"What do you mean, nice? She put you and me in the same category. Tenacity, grit, and all that."

"Grit wasn't one of the words she used."

"Whatever. You know what I'm saying."

Erin scoops her hair up into a giant frizzy ponytail. "C'mon, Ethan, be honest. You have to admit you're surprised. I mean, the desk-evator was imaginative, I'll give you that, but the kids who go to these camps are super-serious inventors. They don't use duct tape."

"Hey!" I throw up my arms. "Unsportsmanlike conduct."

"Well, if you want to make sports analogies, this is the big leagues, not the minors."

"Okay, it's big! I got that part. You said it twenty-five times! But you got invited, and your experiment didn't exactly work, did it?"

She narrows her eyes, points at me. "Don't go there.

I don't need to be reminded of what happened."

Right before Invention Day, Brian and I were playing football on the driveway and he missed a catch. The ball slammed into the table in the garage where Erin's and Zoe's experiment was set up. All their work got ruined, and Erin stopped talking to me for a while, but then one of their solutions kinda worked. Only they couldn't figure out which one, and their display board at Invention Day was about their accidental, unfinished discovery and people who failed at first but then succeeded later. Which they plan to do next year.

Erin taps a finger on her chin. "I wonder why Ms. Gilardi didn't nominate Parneeta. Maybe because she already won Invention Day? Or Naomi. Her antibiotic bandage was very well designed. Or Veronica—"

I wave a hand in front of Erin's face. "She nominated *me*."

Erin takes a rubber band from her wrist and puts it around the index cards. "Yes."

"You want to name some other people who should've been nominated instead?"

She shrugs. "It just seems—"

"You know what? Lots of people think duct tape is an

amazing invention all on its own! Look *that* up, why don't you? Astronauts once used it to fix their moon buggy. On the *moon*, okay!"

I run up the stairs two at a time, then slam my door. I'd bet my entire penny jar that some desperate kid at one of those camps used duct tape for *something*.

ERIN

My treasure hunt will lead Mom and Dad directly to THE INVITATION, which is on the floor in my closet, right by the trifold display board that Zoe and I made for Invention Day. A perfect spot, don't you think?

At last they're home. The wait was excruciating. I march into the kitchen and clap loudly. "Attention, please. I have something extremely important that I need you to do." I hand the first index card to Mom.

She reads it aloud. "'Start in the place that's a spider lair. Look high, look low, for a game that once had air.'" She knits her brows. "What is this, Erin?"

"A treasure hunt! This card will lead you to the next one."

Dad looks over Mom's shoulder. "Can't this wait until after dinner? It's been a long day."

"No. It cannot wait. You'll understand why in a few minutes."

Dad takes the card. "'Start in the place that's a spider lair'? What's that supposed to mean?"

Mom shakes her head. "I have no idea."

Ethan's bouncing a ball against a wall in the family room. "It's the basement. Spiders. Dad's old air hockey table."

"You can't help! Keep quiet!" I make a lock-and-throw-away-the-key motion near my mouth. Ethan rolls his eyes.

Mom and Dad go down to the basement. A minute later they return with clue number two, which was taped to the air hockey table: *Check the space where clothes get dry. You're one step closer to finding out why.*

They head toward the laundry room, then come back with the third clue, which was, of course, in the dryer. *Crystal and glass, please take care. Look for a clue hidden somewhere.*

Dad sighs. "How many more clues are there, Erin?"

I cross my arms. "Just one."

"Where is it?" Ethan asks, after they go into the dining room.

"The treasure? I'm not telling you."

He tries to balance the ball on his head. "I bet I could find it without the clues."

I shoot him a threatening look. "Don't even."

I hear Dad exclaim, "There it is!" He reads the last clue. "'In a room up high behind a door, you'll find a surprise that will make you soar.'"

"Nice rhyme," Ethan comments.

Mom and Dad go upstairs. I hear them opening and closing doors, until at last I think they're in my room. I hear the closet door open. Then silence. Nothing. You could hear a pin drop in this house.

They come down. Mom's holding the invitation, staring at it like she doesn't get it. Sometimes this family is just beyond my understanding.

"Hello!" I cry. "I HAVE BEEN INVITED TO A ZAK CANZERI INNOVATION CAMP!"

"Is this legit?" Mom asks. "Not some scam?"

I stamp my foot. "Oh my God! No! What planet are you living on?"

"I think I've heard of these," Dad says. "A maker-space kind of thing?"

"That's the gist," I say. "But so much more. If you're invited to a ZCIC, it's like being chosen, okay? They only take the best of the best."

Dad whistles, but Mom's still squinting at the invitation. "Who is this Z? How did they get your name? I don't understand."

"He's a brilliant and famous techpreneur! He coined that term, in fact, and Ms. Gilardi nominated me. Mom, this is a once-in-a-lifetime opportunity. I've already looked into it online. You invent something and create it in *five* days. Can you imagine? Either an actual, physical model, a blueprint, or a virtual simulation. You analyze the market and come up with a business plan. Then you present to *actual* potential investors."

"Wow," Mom says, hugging me. "Erin, we're extremely proud. As always."

"Ditto," Dad says. "You are one impressive girl."

I raise an eyebrow. "Woman."

He grins. "Woman."

"Thank you. So I can go, right?"

"We'll check it out, but of course," Mom says. "If it's everything you say it is, then absolutely."

Ethan's been quiet this whole time. He puts the ball down, then pulls a folded, crumpled piece of paper from the back pocket of his jeans. Did you hear that? FOLDED! CRUMPLED!

"Hey, so, yeah, I was invited too."

Mom and Dad turn toward him in slow motion. "You were?" Mom says.

"Unless someone forged this." He hands Dad the paper. "Surprise. A second treasure."

Mom tilts her head. "The same teacher nominated you as well?"

"She nominated five people from McNutt," I explain. "Me, Zoe, Ethan, Brian, and Marlon Romanov, hiss, boo."

Dad strokes his beard. "You know, Eth. Don't feel like you have to prove anything to us. You did Invention Day, and that was great. You tried something different, went out of your comfort zone, and we commend you for that."

Ethan grabs the invitation, stuffs it back into his pocket. "Ms. Gilardi said I have tenacity."

"That's quite a compliment," Mom says.

"She said we *all* have tenacity," I interrupt.

My brother picks up the ball. "I might go."

I stare at him. "You can't be serious."

He gives me a steely look. "Why not? Why can't I be serious?"

"Because," I say. "You're . . . you."

CHAPTER SEVEN

Little Things, Big Things

ZOE

After dinner, Mom puts on her pajamas, gets into bed, and turns on the TV. She's been doing that a lot, almost every night. She says it's the cold, the snow, her new boss at work—everything's making her tired.

I hesitate, then go into her room. "Mom? Can I talk to you about something?"

She lifts a hand but doesn't look away from the TV. "Whatever it is, Zoe, it has to wait until tomorrow. I don't have two brain cells to rub together right now."

I step back. "Oh."

She sinks into her pillow. "Sorry, honey."

"It's all right. I can tell you tomorrow. But definitely tomorrow, okay? It's important. Really important."

She nods, pulls up the covers, closes her eyes.

I look at her for a minute, then go out. I guess this gives me a chance to finish my reasons. I wasn't exactly done, anyway. I actually have two lists, one for Mom and one for me. See what you think.

Five reasons I should go to the camp (the list for Mom):

1. Erin and I could continue our crucial invasive plant research, unless there's a rule you can't work on something you've entered in a previous competition. If there is, I can brainstorm something else to save the environment, which I don't have to tell you is in grave and imminent danger. We're running out of time! We must come up with solutions, and fast.

2. This is an opportunity I might not have again. Ms. Gilardi chose me after considering many others.

3. Hannah needs some mother-daughter bonding time without me around.

4. (Working on it.)

5. (Also working on it.)

Five reasons I should go to the camp (my
private list):

1. Aunt Marci won't miss me, and neither will
my uncle and cousins, who'll be watching
football and screaming at the TV the whole
time, not to mention creating a lot of
garbage.

2. Hannah can talk. And talk. And talk.

3. Ethan will be there.

4. Dad.

5. To clarify the above, because of what Dad
told me the last time we went to the nature
center together.

Bonus reason: Maybe he could come ~~home~~
here and, if they allow it, watch me present
on the last day.

I try to think of reasons four and five on the list
for Mom, but I can't focus. Hannah's singing loudly—

the same song over and over—and Mom's doing this whistling-humming kind of breathing.

I peek into her room. She's asleep. I turn off the TV and her light, then tell Hannah to get ready for bed. She pulls off her headphones and sticks her tongue out at me.

Without a glance outside, I pull down our shade. I used to look out every night and try to identify constellations and think about how ancient people navigated with only the stars as their guide. I wondered if I would've been able to do that, to find where to go without my phone or a map.

I don't gaze at the stars anymore, though. Did you know the name Dara means "evening star"? I looked it up after I found out Dad was staying there with her. I like to know the meanings of names. Zoe means "life" in Greek.

Dara shouldn't have changed my view of the awesome, luminous balls of gas that are quadrillions of miles away, but she did.

Little things are usually what alter big things.

BRIAN

Mom, Dad, and John went to a cultural fair at his school—John helped with the Poland booth—and they left me in charge of Gram. She had to move in with us because she can't remember what day it is or if she brushed her teeth. I can tell you that even if she did brush her teeth, she didn't do a great job.

I'm sleeping in John's room now, but my clothes and stuff are still in my room, where Gram sleeps. It's not easy finding my jeans and shirts in the dark while she's snoring like a jet engine every morning.

Gram's sitting in the one thing Mom let her bring from her apartment—an old blue chair that leans back and has a footstool that pops out. Dad calls it a La-Z-Gram instead of a La-Z-Boy. She's staring at my X-Men poster.

"Hey, Gram." I get last year's yearbook from my bookcase and sit on the floor. Maybe if I was like Professor X, I could read the minds of the girls at McNutt and see if anyone likes me. I flip to last year's sixth-grade pictures. I'm going through every possibility. No more strikeouts.

I run my finger down the rows of names. "Okay, first up, Chloe Carter. She's in my science class. She's cute, but has a weird laugh that sounds like a freaked-out bird. So, no. Second, Kayla Guo. She's a good athlete.

She never talks, though. Not that that's the first thing on my mind."

Gram makes a snorting sound.

"What? I'm just being honest." I go through the pages. "Gwen Larson? Carly Perez? Rafaella Simmons?"

Gram seems to be trying to sit up. I move the lever so the back of the chair pops forward. She reaches for my hand, then covers it with both of hers. Her skin feels like tissue paper.

"Do not push the river," she says.

Gram comes up with these confusing sayings out of nowhere—mostly having to do with things that could kill you—so who knows what this means. "Are you talking about a real river or an imaginary one?" I ask.

She doesn't answer.

"Do not push the river," I repeat. "Okay. Sounds like a plan." I lie on my back and put the yearbook over my face. "Let's face it, I'm hopeless."

Gram makes this laugh-gurgle-type sound. "Oh, Miroslaw."

My dad's name. I take the yearbook off my face. "Gram? I'm Brian."

"Like I always tell you, Miro, spit in the wind and your troubles are gone."

"What? Like really spit?"

And, yeah, I look up and Gram's churning the saliva around in her mouth. Before I can roll away, she hurls a spit onto the carpet. Misses me by an inch, I swear.

Nice. My own grandma just spit at me. Or my dad.

She looks off in the distance; then her eyes start to close, and a minute later she's asleep. I gotta tell you, and this might be rude to say, but oldness = weirdness.

When Mom, Dad, and John get home, along with a hundred relatives who went to see John's Poland booth, Mom makes coffee and has babka and paczki already set out on trays. Two hours of eating and drinking and people yelling and arguing. It's tons of fun.

After the party's over, I go into the dining room, where Dad's finishing his coffee. I should tell him about the camp invitation that everyone but me thinks is a big deal, but Mom shrieks loudly from the kitchen.

"Marta! What are you doing? Did you just spit on the floor?"

I run in, and sure enough, there's a pool of spit in

front of Gram, who's sitting at the table. Man, she's got a lot of spit. Mom wipes it up with a paper towel, muttering in Polish.

I'll tell ya, if I ever get something going with Chloe or Kayla or Gwen or Carly or Rafaella, or anyone else, I'm *never* inviting them to my house. The spit house. They'd run out of here so fast, I wouldn't even get up to bat.

CHAPTER EIGHT

Armor

M.R.

"Your son is exceptional. I believe he is gifted."

The words my preschool teacher spoke to my parents. I remember the exact day. We were in the classroom after the other children had left, and I was standing by the window. It was sunny but raining. Warm, humid, tropical-feeling. I was counting and analyzing the patterns of raindrops on the glass.

Dad, in his dark suit and tie, sitting on a little wooden chair, his wide hands covering his knees, asked: "What does that mean, exactly?"

As if it was a troublesome diagnosis.

The teacher explained how I grasped concepts quickly. That I asked questions beyond what a four-year-old would ask. I knew and used words like "comparison" and "multitude." She recommended that I be tested.

I took it all in. The quiet drips of water streaming into a puddle on the horizontal metal frame. Dad standing, smoothing his pants. Mom fingering the edge of her white sweater. My teacher tipping her head slightly, looking at them quizzically. "This is wonderful," she said. "This is remarkable."

"I suspected as much," Dad answered, glancing in my direction. "My younger brother is like that. Maybe that's where Marlon gets it from. I don't know. But I have to tell you, my brother's an odd guy. Real quirky. Always was. In school the kids excluded him. It didn't matter how brilliant he was; he didn't have any friends. I don't want that to happen to my son. I don't want him to be exceptional."

"But he is," the teacher said softly. "And it's different now. We stress kindness and acceptance. There are programs—"

Dad shook his head, politely said, "Thank you for your time," and motioned for me and Mom to leave. He took my hand, covered it with his, and led me to the car. He was silent on the ride home, so we were too.

I didn't go back to that preschool. The rest of that year, Mom bought me workbooks and puzzles and games, which I devoured at a rapid pace. Then we moved, and she got busy with her job as Dad's social planner.

McNutt is the fifth school I have attended. They're all the same. The teachers tell my parents I'm highly intelligent but seem bored in class. The kids keep their distance, averting their eyes. I prefer being at home, which never feels like a home. What Dad didn't want to happen ended up happening anyway.

He tried to stop it, and with good intentions, I suppose. Some Sundays he took me to baseball games, the zoo, a loud, massive amusement park with rides and shows—always asking if I wanted to "invite a friend."

Dad's smart—not like me, but in a different way. You'd think he'd know that you can't alter someone's genetic makeup with a ride on a roller coaster.

It's all right, though. Two schools ago, I started bringing my Shakespeare volume with me to lunch. It was easier that way. The book is heavy and large; I like to think of it as a sort of armor. I have read through it twice. I'm a fast reader, and I have a lot of time.

Dad was thrilled that I entered Invention Day this

year and last year, because "regular" kids were partici-
pating, not geniuses.

And that is how I will convince him to let me go to
ZCIC.

Ethan Marcus and Brian Kowalski have been invited.
Dad thought their standing-desk invention was a "hoot."
And when they performed their rap song for the crowd at
Invention Day, he was smiling and clapping along.

I know exactly what I will do. I will tell Dad they are
my friends.

CHAPTER NINE

The Museum

ETHAN

Saturday morning, Mom announces we're going on a Marcus family field trip. And the destination is—even hearing the word makes me tired—a museum.

I moan, "Why?" at the same time Erin shouts, "Yay!"

There's me and my sister, both responding with three-letter words ending in y, and that's where the similarities stop.

Mom raises an eyebrow at me. "Because it'll be fun, and informative, and interesting. No arguments, please."

I don't even have time for a bowl of cereal, because we're piled in the car minutes later. Dad tosses me a granola bar while Mom's reading the museum website on her phone and telling us about the exhibits. Erin's like, "Wow! Sounds amazing! Cool. I can't wait to see that!" To be honest, for me it's not only the tiredness factor.

After an hour of looking at the millions of things in those little glass cases, I'm kinda done.

We get there, park a mile from the building. Then Dad buys the tickets. The guy at the counter looks from me to Erin. "Are you guys twins?"

"No!" we both answer. Why does everyone always ask that? We look nothing alike. Erin's a little chubby and short and has crazy frizzy hair, and I'm tall and skinny like Dad, with regular hair.

Mom smiles. "Eleven months apart." She loves to tell people that. Sometimes she describes how Erin was a difficult birth and I was an easy one, but thankfully, she doesn't go into that now.

Right before we go through the turnstile, Mom says, "Hold on a sec. Dad and I wanted to bring you here today because"—she pauses to beam at us—"well, we looked into the camp, and we thought our future techpreneurs could get some inspiration."

Erin stares at her, then gasps. "What are you saying? I can for sure go?"

Mom and Dad nod and Erin, like, gurgles. "This is one of the happiest moments of my life!" she cries.

Dad pats my shoulder. "You can go too, Ethan, but we want to make sure you're fully committed. It's a lot more work than Invention Day."

"Of course we support you," Mom says, "but I admit, we're wondering why you'd want to do this, exactly. Before the desk invention, you never had an interest in science or making things."

"Really," Erin adds. "If you weren't so fidgety in school and hadn't had your little outburst in LA, Invention Day would never have been on your radar."

I push the turnstile roughly. "Thanks, everyone."

Erin's right behind me. "Ethan, the kids at these camps are so far and above. You should look at the website. What they make is incredible. And, well, I'll be immersed in my own project, so I won't be able to"—she makes air quotes—"*save* you this time."

That was a foul. A technical! She should be thrown out of the museum. Or the family. One thing about my sister—she never forgets anything. How many times is she going to bring up the fact that she, quote, unquote, "saved" me with the stand-in during LA and got Mr. Delman to consider the standing desk idea?

"Don't worry! You won't have to *save* me!" I shout, making air quotes too.

Some woman turns around, and Mom touches my arm. "Inside voice, hon."

"Maybe we should revisit this later," Dad says, leading us into the first exhibit. The three of them walk through an arched doorway, and I sort of huff and stomp after them. I don't know if I'm huffing and stomping because I'm mad about what they said or because I think what they said is true.

The exhibit is on the Wright brothers—Orville and Wilbur, the guys who invented, built, and flew the first plane. Mom, Dad, and Erin start listening to a guy in a brown shirt and the same color brown pants. He's standing near a full-size model of their airplane and talking about aerodynamics and gravity and velocity. It looks more like a giant kite than an airplane, if you ask me.

I wander around the exhibit, looking at the stuff in the cases, then stop in front of a bicycle. There's a sign that says it's a replica of the type of bicycle the Wright brothers rode. Turns out—and I never knew this—the bros weren't engineers or scientists or even high school graduates.

They repaired and sold bicycles. The plaque says people with a lot more cred tried to fly a plane and failed. But O and W kept trying and finally figured it out. They studied birds and the wind and kites. And, weirdly, bicycles.

Okay, here's a secret about me: I never learned to ride a bike. Dad never did either when he was a kid, and neither of us can Rollerblade or skateboard. He says the Marcus men are missing a wheels gene.

Mom taps my back and says we're moving on to the next exhibit. We must go to at least ten others, but all through the day I can't stop thinking about the bicycle.

When we get home, I go into the garage and pull out the bike Mom and Dad bought for my tenth birthday. (Dad was hoping the gene had skipped me.) It's dusty, but otherwise in good shape. I think I gave up on it after a few weak, half-hearted attempts.

I wheel it out to the sidewalk, fasten my helmet, and get on. Then this is how the next twenty minutes go: me pedaling, trying to balance, falling. Repeat, repeat, repeat. My palms get scraped, one knee is bleeding, and I rip my shirt, but like the fiftieth time I get on, I make it halfway down the block before I lose my balance.

And it's a crazy-good feeling.

I jump off and grab the bike before it hits the ground. The whole time, those few seconds, all I could think about was Orville and Wilbur, and how they were smarter than the most brilliant scientists. Because they studied *normal* stuff. How birds use their wings and how kites stay in the air. And how bicycles work!

I run home, wheeling the bike, and then drop it in the garage. I rush inside, realize I'm still wearing my helmet. "I rode my bike!"

Erin, Mom, and Dad look at me like I'm nuts.

"You rode your bike?" Mom repeats.

"I did it! I made it half a block!" I shout. "And you know what else? I got inspiration! I'm going to the camp!"

Erin spits out some water she's drinking. "Wait, wait. Just because you finally rode a bike doesn't mean you'll survive at the camp. Ethan, I urge you to really think about this—"

"I have! Two regular guys with no science background, just their instinct, get a plane to fly, okay? What about that!"

They all seem too stunned (or confused) to answer.

"You're talking about the Wright brothers?" Dad asks as Mom gives me a paper towel to blot my knee.

I ball it up in my hand. "Yes! Don't you always say we can do anything we put our minds to? Gilardi has confidence in me. She said she considered *lots* of kids. But she picked me!"

Brian has to be wrong! We're not the slacker examples. They wouldn't intentionally do that to a kid, would they? Set someone up like that? I know I'm not like Erin or Romanov or probably all the usual kids who get invited to these camps, but if two guys who fixed bikes could get a plane to fly, why can't I invent a desk-evator that works? A new and improved version, in fact! Without duct tape this time.

"There's something else," I say. "Something that might not seem big, but is. Every invention needs one basic ingredient—someone who believes in it and stands behind it. In my case, literally. I'm going. I'm finishing what I started. I want to see it through."

Dad nods firmly. "You have my vote." Mom smiles and applauds. "Okay!"

Erin stares at me. "No. This is *not* okay."

I groan. "For once in your life, could you have some faith in me?"

She sighs. "That's not it. I'm . . . I just . . . don't want you to be embarrassed again."

"I wasn't embarrassed!" An 89 percent lie. Well, maybe closer to 95.

"Ethan, listen to me. At Invention Day . . . people were laughing at you behind your back. Saying mean things. I told them to stop, but you know how people are."

"No, they weren't! I didn't see anyone laughing. I didn't hear anything."

She bites her lip, shakes her head.

I swallow. She's serious. I unbuckle my helmet, take it off, hold it in my hands.

"Sorry."

"Whatever," I mutter.

Erin looks down. "There's something else I have to tell you."

"What? Someone made a meme of me that went viral?"

"No . . . it's the report for Mrs. D'Antonio. Now that

all this has happened, I've been thinking that we—I—need to put the report on hold for the time being."

"What do you mean? The camp isn't for a couple of weeks. You have time to finish it."

"No. I need to put all my mental energy toward my project for ZCIC. I have to prepare."

"You promised."

"Yes, I feel bad about that. I shouldn't have."

"But you did."

Mom and Dad are letting us argue, working it out on our own like they'd usually advise. But there is no working it out. Erin promises (again) that she'll get back to the report "sometime in January" and says that might be better anyway, to present it to Mrs. D after winter break, when she's all fresh and rested, and besides . . .

She keeps talking.

I stop listening.

After a few minutes Mom and Dad both doze off, which proves my point about museums. (Or, actually, it could be the droning of Erin's voice.) I leave while she's still going. In the garage, I prop my bike against the wall and hang the helmet on the handlebars.

Now that Erin's two bombs have been dropped, my crazy-good feeling from riding the bike just feels crazy, minus the good. Maybe Erin's right. Maybe Gilardi's delusional. All those lab chemicals affected her brain or something.

I kick one of the pedals and it spins around. Am I doing this or not? It's like there's a cartoon angel and devil floating above my shoulders, except one is Erin, saying *"You?"* and the other side is Orville and Wilbur, saying "Why *not* you? Missing a wheels gene and you rode a bike, didn't you?"

I stand there for a while, looking at the bike. Then something occurs to me. I bet people said mean things and laughed at O and W while they tried to fly their giant kite. Doubted they could do it. Said they'd never survive.

But they did.

And you know what? I also bet that the first model they made wasn't all that amazing.

CHAPTER TEN

Shocks

ZOE

Mom's standing at our front window, her arms crossed. "The woodpecker's back."

Hannah rushes toward her, doing a few off-balance leaps. "Where?"

I come over too, as Mom points. "Same spot on the mailbox. Why can't he find a tree like other woodpeckers?"

A black-feathered woodpecker with a red crown has been hanging out on the side of our mailbox, pecking away for most of the weekend. He's made a hole the size of a quarter. Our mailbox looks like a little house, with shingles and a roof. I think he's claimed it as his home and is getting ready to move in.

Mom opens the front door and claps her hands loudly a few times. The bird pays no attention. "Should I tape up the hole? I don't want him to nest in there."

Hannah squeals as the woodpecker squeezes inside the mailbox. "Look! Too late! He went in!"

Mom closes the door. "Now what? Should I call an animal service?"

"No!" I cry. "Like many species, woodpeckers are losing their natural habitats. He's adapting. We're witnessing adaptation right in front of us! If he thinks our mailbox is a good home, what's wrong with it?"

"We get our mail there, that's what wrong with it," Mom says. "It'll be full of bird poop."

Hannah flops onto Dad's favorite chair, which is still here, next to the sofa. Mom won't move it, but she won't sit in it either.

"I bet he wants to find a girl woodpecker and then they'll have baby woodpeckers," Hannah says, swinging her legs and pulling a long string of gum out of her mouth.

Mom sinks onto the sofa. "Actually."

I frown, sit next to her. "Actually, what?" Her face is so not good. Seems like every day she looks more tired than the day before.

"Your dad and . . . Dara are expecting a baby," Mom says.

I clutch my heart. "How do you know? Did you talk to him?"

"He sent me an e-mail."

Hannah jumps up. "I'm going to have a little sister?"

Mom closes her eyes for a second, then opens them. "Or a brother. He didn't say much. Except that the baby's due in June. And they're . . . getting married."

So Dad really is staying there. For good. Doesn't he miss us? Has he forgotten about us? We were his family first.

"Did Dad ask about me?" I say. Mom shakes her head.

Hannah's oblivious, chattering about names she's going to suggest to Dad for the baby. She's counting them off on her fingers. "Ava, Charlotte, Isabella . . ."

How can I bring up the camp now? I've been waiting for the right moment, when Mom isn't tired or distracted, but that hasn't happened. I need to ask anyway. It feels like this news is another reason to go, except it belongs on my list, not the list to persuade Mom.

She's staring off into space. I clear my throat. "Mom, this might not be a good time, but what I needed to talk to you about the other night . . ."

"Yes, I forgot. What is it?"

"Well, amazing news, actually. I've been invited to a prestigious technology camp. Ms. Gilardi, the eighth-grade science teacher, nominated only five kids from McNutt, and I'm one of them. It's very selective. You design something, make it yourself, then do a whole presentation on the last day. Erin was invited too. I really, really want to go. Can I?"

"It sounds great. When is it?"

"Over winter break."

"When, exactly?"

"Um, that's the thing. It's the week we're visiting Aunt Marci. But this is such a tremendous opportunity. Erin said I could stay at her house We could continue our plant research if they let us, and you could have some one-on-one time with Hannah."

Hannah blows a giant bubble, then pops it on her nose. "Cool."

Mom puts a hand on my knee. "Zoe, you can't miss the visit."

"But—"

"I'm sorry to disappoint you, but no. It's out of the question." She twists her mouth. "They're the only family who care about us. You can go to the camp another time."

"No, you don't understand. It's not like that. They don't have them often and you—"

She gets up and walks into the kitchen, and I know that's it. Hannah sings, "Too bad, you can't go," and I run into my room and slam the door. It feels like what Dad told me will never come true now. This was my chance. This was the first real step toward my dream. And it's crushed, like bits of awful, landfilling Styrofoam.

I grab my phone and text Erin. **My mom said no!!!**

MAJORLY UPSET, she replies.

She won't even consider the camp. I have to visit my aunt. My fingers can't bear to type the other news, about Dad.

I'll keep you in the loop remotely, Erin says. **I'll text you whenever I can. I'll sneak into the bathroom if I have to. Even though I heard they're super strict about texting.**

This actually makes me smile. **Erin Marcus?** I say. **Breaking a rule?**

When necessary, yes.

Thanks.

Of course! We're in this together, whether you're there or not.

I type a few hearts and she responds with a smiley face.

My shade is pulled down. I can't see the mailbox, but I can still hear the woodpecker. His taps sound like a tiny jackhammer. Did you know the woodpecker's beak is designed to absorb the shock and protect its brain?

I wish people had something built-in like that to absorb shocks.

Because right now my brain feels sad and mushy all over.

CHAPTER ELEVEN

The Countdown

BRIAN

I text Ethan on Sunday night: I'm out.

His reply: I figured.

I didn't even tell my parents. I'm turning in my drill.

We never used a drill.

All the more reason. I might've had to. U going?

At least a full minute goes by; then he says, I think so.

I have no words. All I can type is: ?????!!!!!

I know.

U sure?

No.

Then why?

I don't want to give up. I got inspired by something. Or someone. Two someones.

Who?

The Wright brothers.

The plane guys?

Yeah.

I'm not even gonna ask. But pleez tell me you're not doing the DE again. You're making something else, right?

I am.

Good.

The NEW AND IMPROVED DE.

What? R U CRAZY?

Probably.

Okay. Now that that's cleared up. How u gonna make it new & improved?

Working on that part.

Sounds real solid so far.

Another pause, and then Ethan goes, Is it true people were saying mean things and laughing at us at ID? Erin said so.

It's true.

Why didn't you tell me?

Would you have told you?

Good point.

Well, here's my advice, I say. If you insist on going

ahead with your new and improved version, don't use any materials from your kitchen.

Done.

Then best of luck, dude. You're gonna need it.

Thanks.

No doubt in my mind. He's gonna die there.

M.R.

No, I've never been bullied, if that's what you're wondering. Not in the traditional sense. But there's something else that kids do, and it's just as bad in a way. They look beyond you. Around you. Even through you, like you're invisible.

That wasn't the case all the time in every school. There were some polite kids, even nice ones. A few acquaintances who might've become friends. But then we moved.

When I arrived at McNutt last year, I started going to the media center after I finished my lunch. I like the quiet, neat rows of books. In alphabetical order, and protected with plastic. Usually no one else is there.

I told Dad my friends were going to the innovation camp and they were regular kids, not geniuses. He sent in the registration and check the next day.

"Try not to say things that put the other kids off," he told me. "It's easy. Be one of the guys. Smile a lot; shake hands; talk about sports. Or the weather, that's always a good topic."

Like he does.

Mom says gifted people have trouble with "social cues" and "nuances." She's been trying to help me learn to detect them, when she has time and isn't hosting a dinner for Dad's important clients.

She explained that people don't usually say exactly what they're thinking, and you have to watch their gestures and expressions.

I described to Mom what happened at last year's Invention Day, when I told Erin Marcus that men were better than girls at science. It was a logical fact. All three of the winners were boys, including me, who placed first.

"Why was she mad?" I asked.

"That wasn't a nice thing to say. You insulted her. She's a girl."

"But it was true."

"It doesn't matter if it was true. She felt offended."

"Why?"

"You hurt her feelings, most likely."

"But how?"

Mom sighed. "Just don't say things like that."

You know what my first idea is for an invention at ZCIC? Something for kids like me to detect nuances and social cues.

How could I even make something like that? It would have to be magic.

Even if you're gifted, you're not magic.

ERIN

Monday morning before the bell rings, I'm at my locker. It's right next to Ethan's. He's leafing through papers in a folder, and Brian's leaning against the opposite wall, staring at every girl who walks by.

Ethan groans. "No, not again. I forgot my social studies homework. For the third time this year. Just send me to Reflection right now."

Brian laughs. "You know what you need? A homework alarm. No, more like a freakin' siren attached to your head."

Ethan slams his locker door. "Very funny. What excuse do I come up with this time? I already used 'my mom accidentally threw it away' and 'my computer crashed.'"

Brian goes, "How about your dog peed on it? Oh yeah, you don't have a dog." They walk off together, Brian continuing to laugh and Ethan continuing to groan.

Typical. And I can tell you exactly where his homework is. One of two places: on the beanbag in his room or on the kitchen counter, right by where he drops his backpack on the floor every day after school. He's visually challenged in the morning, I think.

I grab my stuff and hurry to my first class. Brian's right—my brother does need a homework alarm. Ugh, did I just think that Brian's *right* about something? That's a first. Suddenly I stop in the middle of the hall. Wait, wait, wait. Forgetting homework . . . excuses . . . an alarm . . . Is it actually possible that Brian "everything's a joke" Kowalski just gave me an idea for ZCIC?

I duck into science, find my seat, and flip open my spiral. This is not at all Erin-style, but I scribble notes for the entire class period instead of paying attention.

Forgetting homework. Missed assignments. Being

unprepared for tests. Lower grades. Failure! A vicious
circle! But what if you had something that wouldn't let
you forget your homework! Real-time. Virtual. A con-
stant reminder. Fun to use.

By the end of fourth period I've got several pages of
notes to myself. And that's just what I'll call my invention: Note to Self. Or NTS.

OMG! TIG! (This Is Good!)

I grab Zoe's arm as she's heading into the cafeteria
for lunch. "Media center, you and me," I say. "Right now."

She looks worried. "What's the matter?"

"I'll tell you when we get there."

You're allowed to eat lunch in the media center if you
(1) are quiet and (2) have work to do. Both rules apply.

We sit at a table and spread out our lunches. "Zoe,
first, I'm really sorry you can't go to the camp," I say.

"Yeah. Me too. This'll take a while to get over."

"I know, and that's why I want to keep you involved.
I had a lightning bolt of an idea this morning, and you're
the first person I'm going to tell. Lightning bolt—did you
see how I worked in Z's logo?"

She nods, then looks down. "Invasive plants?"

"No. I would never go ahead without you!"

She smiles, peels open her yogurt. "Okay, tell me everything."

"So, Ethan forgot his homework *again* today, and Brian made a joke about Ethan needing a homework alarm, and it hit me. What if kids really did have some sort of reminder alarm?"

"Makes sense. Go on."

"Enter the NTS. Note to Self. The all-in-one homework reminder, assignment tracker, and anti-failure guarantee." I flip through my pages of notes. "Still fleshing out the details, but it would be like a bracelet or something that's synched to your teachers' web pages. A wearable device that would buzz with reminders of when things are due and provide links, even video, always keeping you on track so you never miss anything. Ding, do your math homework. Ding, study for that LA test. Ding, you're in the honor society." I let out a long breath. "What do you think?"

Her eyes get a little teary. "I think it's great! You'd just have to make sure that kids couldn't disable it."

"You're right!" I jot that down.

"And maybe you could build in some sort of reward system? Like in a video game? Earn gold coins or candy?"

"Another excellent point. See, you can be a part of this."

Zoe blinks and sniffles a little. "Thanks."

The door swings open and guess who walks in? Marlon. He goes over to the farthest table, sits down, and opens that huge book he always has at lunch. I push up the lead on my mechanical pencil. *Just ignore him,* I tell myself.

INE. It's Not Easy. But I do my best.

Later, when I get home, I get right to work. I make a poster to count down the days leading up to ZCIC. I've called it Z Minus, paying homage to the term "T minus," which is used for the time prior to a rocket launch. Clever, don't you think?

There's so much to do! I'll need to research coding, electronic devices, microcontrollers, and existing homework/study apps to see how they can be improved. Plus there's the whole business side of things. And logos! Design! This is for sure *big.* My device could be used in schools *everywhere.*

Much to my concern, my brother has announced he's

definitely going. I advised him to take this seriously, but as I said before, he's him.

A few days later, our information packets arrive. Except they're called Zackets. Inside there's a welcome letter from Z, signed "Zincerely yours," with a big, scrawled gold Z. Don't you love that? They've really got their brand down.

I read everything thoroughly, including Z's bio. It's even more amazing than I thought! He's got several "groundbreaking initiatives" in the works, including a lotion that will be able to detect when a mole turns suspicious and could become skin cancer. Z has received millions in start-up funding for the project. But still he gives his time to mentor the future generation. Wow, just wow.

You will not be surprised when I tell you that Ethan's Zacket has remained on the kitchen counter, untouched and unopened.

I make index cards with highlighted notes and arrange them neatly around my room, keeping my door closed at all times. I don't need any leaks to you-know-who, in case Ethan decides to ask for advice, like he did with the desk-evator.

I decide to wear my black holiday skirt and a light blue sweater on the first day so I look polished and professional but not like I'm trying too hard to impress. I'll have to borrow Mom's black heels, even though they're a little big on me.

My hair is the issue. But by experimenting with a combination of gels, creams, and mousses, I'm able to get it to stay down and neat, held back into a bun at the nape of my neck.

Everything is lining up perfectly.

I've got it this time, Marlon.

ETHAN

The Orville and Wilbur side won. I tried the bike again, and rode it around the block! The crazy-good feeling came back, and this time it was all good, minus the crazy.

I hope the crazy part doesn't resurface, because I'm going. I am *going*. I'm doing this.

I know, for starters, I need to open the packet. And as I figured, there's way too much to go through. What to bring, how to get there, what to expect, how to prepare.

Tons of paper, including a whole page on a one-minute introductory speech you have to do on the first day, talking about yourself, your goals, and your accomplishments "thus far."

One minute? I could cover that in ten seconds.

Ethan Marcus, seventh grader. Decent at volleyball. I forget my homework and get fidgety sitting in school. I'm here because I made a desk-evator out of spatulas and a cutting board. Don't laugh.

Erin comes into the kitchen. "Oh, good, you're finally going through the packet." She grabs a mini box of raisins from the pantry. "Listen, I've been meaning to tell you. You should borrow Dad's dress shoes. I'm going to wear Mom's heels so I look professional."

"Really?"

She rolls her eyes. "If you're doing this, get with the program. DFA."

"Huh?"

"Don't Fool Around."

"Do they talk with initials at the camp or something?"

She just says, "Ethan," then goes back upstairs.

Dad's *shoes*? I put everything back into the envelope,

then go into Dad's closet and slip on the black shoes Erin's talking about. First, they're too big on me. Second, they're the most uncomfortable shoes I've ever put on. And third, I can already tell they're gonna make my feet sweat. I pull them off and put them back. No way. I'm not wearing those, no matter what Erin says.

I hear my sister's voice coming from her room, loud and clear, like she has a megaphone. Sounds like she's practicing her speech. Her door's been closed constantly. Once, when she was at Zoe's, I went in there. She had about a hundred index cards in piles on the floor with highlighted headings: *Product, Design, Market, Strategy, Financials.* Like usual, like her whole life, my sister is organized/prepared/scary/light-years ahead of me.

Not so much going on in my room. The new and improved DE remains solidly in the idea phase. And it hangs out there for a while.

Finally it's the last day of school before winter break. We're watching movies in class, but still the day is going by painfully slow. Like the end of an NBA game with all the time-outs.

At last I'm on my way to LA (we won't watch a movie in Delman's class, I can tell you that for sure) when I see Wesley Pinto standing by the bulletin board outside the music room. His hair's a lot longer than when we hung out together (yeah, right) in Reflection, and he's wearing black Converse, not his usual hiking boots. He's tacking a piece of paper to the board. Everyone's always been scared of him—he's so tough-guy all the time—but today he looks different.

I always thought it was Wesley who put an anonymous note in my locker that made me rethink how to build the desk-evator. When I was at my lowest point during the Invention Day crisis and almost quit, a mysterious note appeared in my locker. The desk-evator wasn't a stellar creation, as you know, but the note gave me a clue about making it a different way, with legs that folded in instead of sides that raised up. I never asked Wesley about it. I mean, we're not friends. And I didn't want to risk getting pummeled.

He picks up a stack of papers and a box of thumbtacks from the floor, then walks away. I quickly read the paper—it's a flyer about a band that's playing somewhere after winter break. There's a picture of some guys, including Wesley, who's sitting in front of a drum set. He's in a band now? And he plays the drums? Wow. I wouldn't exactly say this out loud, but I feel kinda happy for him.

Mrs. Slovenko waves to me from the music room, where she's adjusting the height of a black metal music stand. "Have a melodious holiday!" she calls, then opens a book and places it on the stand.

I glance at Wesley's flyer once more, then head to LA. Wouldn't it be funny if he somehow secretly helped me again? Like if there was a clue on the flyer about how to make the desk-evator new and improved? Like that would happen.

Delman's on a continuous roll with his puns, shooting them off like fireworks. Spelling bees and Santa's elves being subordinate clauses and some joke about commas and cats. When the final bell rings, there's a stampede to the door and a mad rush to the buses, but Brian and I decide to walk because there's a heat wave. Twenty-five degrees!

"I can't hang out," he tells me. "My mom's baking

Christmas cookies for the entire Polish universe and I'm the delivery boy." He knocks a fist into my arm as we cut through the park. "Keep in touch, man. Don't ever change."

I do a fake sniffle. "I won't forget you."

"Oh, but you will. I see the writing on the wall. In another week, you're gonna get sucked into that Zak Canzeri world. I'll blink, and you'll be in with all those inventor-business-science people. Can't they decide what to call themselves?"

"Yeah, right. And, not gonna happen."

He grins. "Okay, because you're leaving me in the dust, here's advice number two. You ready?"

"Uh-huh. Lay it on me."

"Spit into the wind."

"What?"

"Gram, she told me that. She's been, like, spitting a lot. It's driving my mom insane, but who knows? Maybe there's some bizarre, unknown reason old people spit."

"Too much saliva?"

"Or they just wanna share a little part of themselves with the world." We get to my house and he turns, walks backward, then shoots out a wad of spit that lands some-where in the snow. "So, you got the new-and-improved thing all worked out?"

"Nah. I'm just gonna wing it. Figure it out when I get there."

Brian laughs. "That's my boy."

Did you catch that swiftly executed pun? *Wing* it.

Stay with me, O and W. I have a feeling I'm gonna need you guys.

CHAPTER TWELVE

Questions

ERIN

Do you know anything about coding? Or "smart objects" that have built-in software, sensors, and network connectivity?

I've come to the conclusion that my skill set is more in the area of planning and strategizing, not programming. One of the most important rules of inventing is knowing what you can and can't do.

I'm at that point. So if you hear of anyone who has knowledge in these subjects, it would be extremely helpful as I move forward. Let me know ASAP. Thx.

ETHAN

Yeah, yeah. I know I can't wear sweatpants to the camp. How clueless do you think I am? I wasn't seriously going to do that. But let me ask you—what about a T-shirt?

Not one with stains or holes, I mean. That'd be okay, right?

BRIAN

I have three. (1) Will a girl, any girl, ever like me? (2) Will I grow taller than four-eleven? Because that would be nice. Say what you want, but in my experience, girls just aren't that into short guys. It's true, okay? I know what I know. And (3) What's gonna happen with Gram?

M.R.

Why aren't people clear, and easy to understand, like things?

ZOE

Can I ask more than one? Is that all right? Because I have a lot.

Will Mom kick the woodpecker out? I think he's made our mailbox his permanent home. Mom let me put out a plastic bin for the mail, but I can tell she's not happy with that solution. If she calls an animal service, where will they take him?

Is our world going to be okay?

How come I always feel like I'm going to cry any second?

Do you think Ethan's going to break up with me? I offered him a drink of my organic mixed-berry juice and he had, like, a spasm. He flailed his arms and shook his head and shouted, "No!" I asked him what was wrong, and this is what he said: "It's just . . . I can't . . . You're too . . ."

That was one of the moments I felt like I was going to cry. Follow-up question: What did he mean?

Will I survive three days of Aunt Marci?

Last one. Does Dad still love me?

Please say yes.

CHAPTER THIRTEEN

And Then We're There

ETHAN

The night before the first day of camp, I have a dream/ nightmare that I'm drowning in Zoe's berry juice and my sister is choking Romanov while Wes and his band are playing. Brian's throwing cookies at the audience, but they turn into Frisbees. Mrs. Slovenko, on lead vocals, keeps raising and lowering the music stand.

Thankfully, when my alarm rings at six thirty, no one's been choked that I know of and I'm on dry land.

I quickly get dressed and go downstairs. The vacuum's out, waiting by the tinsel shreds on the carpet, and Mom's already packing the ornaments in a box. Mom and Dad don't believe in making Christmas a big commercial deal, so we always do a useful family gift. This year it was a plushy new chair for the family room. Are they purposely trying to torment me? A chair. Really, a *chair*?

I walk into the kitchen and get a bowl for cereal; then Erin rushes past and flings open the pantry door. She's got her hair in a little bun, and she's wearing a skirt, a sweater, and Mom's shoes. Plus she's carrying a leather briefcase. She sets it down and whirls around. "Are we out of protein bars?"

"Maybe," I say, knowing I ate the last one.

She eyes me from head to toe. "Is that what you're wearing?"

"Yeah." I decided on jeans and a T-shirt. One of my *nice* T-shirts. Plain blue. And my good jeans.

She sighs. "Remember to take your Zacket. And BYOD, too."

"What?"

"Bring Your Own Device. That was mentioned in the Zacket. Ethan, it's exhausting to keep reminding you of everything."

Dad hurries into the kitchen and says we need to go, that traffic's bad. He's going in late to work because he wants to drive us on the first day. Mom wishes us good luck and hugs us tightly, like we're leaving for a month. "Keep in touch with me."

Erin shakes her head. "Mom, you know they limit texting. I promise I'll give you the full rundown later."

I do a thumbs-up. "I will too. You can count on me to give you the full rundown."

During the ride to Forest Hill, Erin chatters nonstop. It's hot in the car, the sun's bright, and her voice becomes a buzzing background noise that makes me sleepy. I jolt when Dad says, "This is it, guys." I yawn and peer out at a square glass-and-steel building with rows of small, darkened windows on each floor.

Erin leaps out of the car. "It's exactly how I imagined it would be!"

"We're not even inside yet," I comment.

She ignores that. "Could they have chosen a more perfect setting? It's so sleek, so *powerful*."

"It looks like Gotham City."

She motions. "C'mon! What're you waiting for?" She starts marching toward the building, briefcase in hand. "Let the camp begin!"

I slide out and shut the door. Dad lowers the window. "I'll be out front at six."

"Okay."

He leans closer. "Eth. Have fun."

"Thanks, Dad."

I hurry after Erin, who's already opening the door. She disappears inside. When I find her, she's standing in line at the check-in table behind a guy with a cap that says I AM THE FUTURE.

"Look!" Erin squeals, pulling the sleeve of my jacket. She points to a giant black banner above the table with a huge, shiny gold *Z* surrounded by lightning bolts. "We're really here. We're really, really here!"

"Calm down, Erin. Take a breath."

"I'm breathing just fine, thank you. And FYI, no one has ever calmed down when someone told them to calm down."

The guy who is the future leaves; then it's our turn. The woman sitting behind the table has a buzz cut and lots of earrings. "Hi. I'm Maddox. And you are?"

Erin extends her hand. "Erin Marcus. Nice to meet you, Maddox."

I reach out my hand too and Maddox shakes it. "Ethan Marcus," I say.

"Oh, awesome—you guys are twins?" Maddox asks, and we answer at the same time, "No!"

"Sorry about that. Didn't mean to offend. Okay, you're both checked in. You can sit wherever for this morning's Zorientation." She tips her head. "We're starting in the atrium. Go on back. Make yourself at home, peeps."

"Thank you," Erin says, and marches on. I follow my sister through some double doors.

Then it's like we've entered another dimension. Or should I say Zimension? There are a ton of kids in a big room with a high glass ceiling, some wearing jeans and some dressed up like Erin. A few guys have shiny, puffy vests over their shirts. Everyone's sitting at round tables, on their phones or talking. Each table has a smaller version of the gold *Z*-lightning-bolt banner on a stand. Black tablecloths, black chairs. Gold pencils with *Z*s on them.

Erin weaves her way through the tables, and I can think of nothing better to do at this point than to keep following her. She stops at a table with two empty chairs. "Are these taken?" she asks a guy with light brown skin, short curly hair, and round Harry Potter–type glasses.

"All yours," he says. I pull out one of the chairs and sit next to the kid with the I AM THE FUTURE cap. There's also a girl with braids and, like, a hundred bracelets on her arms. She's moving her finger around a tablet screen and doesn't glance up. Two other guys are at the table, looking at their phones.

Erin's shading her eyes and scanning the room. "I don't see him. Do you see him?"

"Who? Z?"

"No, Marlon. Maybe he won't show." She plops down and sticks out her hand to the glasses guy. "Erin Marcus. That's my brother, Ethan. Not twins. Don't ask if we are."

He laughs as he shakes her hand. "Okay. Fair enough. Hi, Erin and Ethan, not twins. I'm Connor."

Bracelet girl and I AM THE FUTURE don't say anything, and neither do the two other guys. It's a little awkward.

Four people (all wearing black clothes, I notice) are standing at the front of the room, including Maddox. One guy says into a microphone: "If you all could find a seat, that would be amazing." After everyone settles down, he goes, "Welcome to the tenth Zak Canzeri Innovation

Camp. My name is Jet, and I'm head of the Z Team. To my left is Asher and to my right is Imani. Most of you met Maddox when you checked in."

"There he is," Erin whispers, and I spot Romanov heading toward the last seat at a table by the front.

"We've personally chosen each of you," Jet's saying, "because we think you have what it takes. You will be—or already are—the future."

The guy with the cap is nodding, like, yeah, he already knew that.

I poke Erin. "Where's Z?"

"I'm sure he doesn't come for the prelim stuff. He's the CEO. Come on. His people handle that."

"During these five days," Jet goes on, "we'll be doing lots of critical thinking, creating, innovating, collaborating, questioning." Asher and Imani, standing with their hands clasped behind their backs, smile briefly. "But at ZCIC we go further than exploration. Because what's exploration without an end result? We rise above. We conquer. We succeed. Simply said, being here"—Jet points to a window—"will get you there."

I lost him about halfway through, but Erin's eyes are

now glazed, and the kid in the cap hasn't stopped nod-ding. Bracelet girl puts her tablet on the table. There's a drawing on it that looks like a kaleidoscope, with pink, purple, and silver swirls and circles.

"Here's the plan for today," Jet says. "We're going to start with a short video, then your intro speeches. Next, there will be four Zations for you to visit. Coding/programming, energy/sustainability, engineering, and robotics. You'll be able to peruse examples of past proj-ects our innovators have made.

"After lunch, Z will join us"—Erin gasps—"and then this afternoon, you'll decide on your project and form a team. Or you may work on your own. Many of you have already begun that phase, which is awesome."

Erin is blowing out little breaths from her mouth. She clutches my arm. "Tell me I'm not imagining this."

Jet waves a hand. "Now, please turn your attention to the front of the room."

A screen drops down and the lights dim; then a giant gold *Z* appears on the screen. The video starts with scenes of kids at previous camps, talking about their inventions and how the "Z experience" changed their lives. Then there's this part about TADA, and how it's woven into everything they do. Tenacity, Appetite, Determination, Aim. There are photos with kids doing their presentations, and a few shots of an awards ceremony. The video ends with the gold Z again, and everyone applauds wildly.

The lights go on; then it's speech time. After the first few kids go, reciting how they analyzed defects in mice cells and made a robot in their spare time (not kidding), Erin's name is called. She says she's "truly honored" to be here, talks about her "previous work" at Invention Day, and says her goal is to become the CEO of her own company one day: EM Industries.

Of course. Figures.

They call me next. I introduce myself, then say, "I have an idea for standing desks in school. I made something but it didn't turn out great so I'm here to make it better." Short and sweet, ten seconds total. Except the glances around me don't look all that impressed.

Bracelet girl, whose name is Natalia, talks about how drawing mandalas—circular diagrams with a pattern— can help calm people on the autism spectrum. She says her brother is autistic and she designed a program to lessen his agitation. Maybe that's what she was doing on her tablet.

When Connor gets up, he talks mostly about his dog and how he likes to cook. Then he mentions "some coding stuff I did."

Next up is Romanov.

He stands straight, arms stiffly at his sides. "Hello. My name is Marlon Romanov. I intend to win."

Whoa.

The room is completely silent for a second; then I hear some snickers and whispers. Romanov says, "My invention . . . ," then stops and abruptly sits down without finishing his sentence.

Maddox laughs and pumps her fist. "Well, *all right.* I admire your honesty."

"He would say that," Erin mutters.

Connor looks at her. "You know that guy?"

"Unfortunately, yes. He goes to my school. We have a history. We are *not* friends, in case you were wondering."

"Hmm, interesting. What's the history?"

"Never mind that," Erin replies, perking up. "So, you code?"

CHAPTER FOURTEEN

Puzzle Piece

M.R.

I said something wrong again, didn't I? I was stating my intention. I want to win and I aim to win. Was I not supposed to express my goal in my speech? There was nothing in the Zacket that prohibited mentioning a goal. Erin Marcus did.

My few words were followed by unpleasant looks. Surprise, disbelief, and perhaps disdain from the people near me. I am not certain. I am never certain. There were some sneers, raised eyebrows, a bit of quiet laughter. I was planning to briefly summarize the idea for my invention, but I quickly returned to my seat.

A girl at my table said: "Well, aren't you all that?"

I didn't understand. All that what?

The other kids at the table looked beyond, around, through.

Mom has told me that exceptional people have trouble fitting into a world that wasn't designed for them. No matter where I am, this seems to be true.

Did you know I like to do jigsaw puzzles? I challenge myself with each new one. A faster time, or more pieces. In the last puzzle I completed (five thousand), there were several uniform-colored pieces that bore no relation to the pieces they fit with. Solid orange, green, black.

Difficult, oddly shaped, nearly impossible to find where they go. Nothing that would indicate how they connect to the pieces around them. Quite frustrating.

As I suspect you realize, I am not referring only to the pieces.

This morning, when I arrived at ZCIC, I envisioned something different. I thought perhaps this time it would be easier to fit into the puzzle. But the kids here seem mostly the same as the kids at McNutt and the other schools.

Them, and me.

I fear it will always be this way.

CHAPTER FIFTEEN

Zations and a Zactivity

ERIN

I think I did okay, but I was nervous during my speech. I could hear my voice shaking slightly. Public speaking is actually one of people's biggest fears, along with going to the dentist. I'm usually so confident and articulate. The nervousness must be due to my elated state of mind. Don't worry. IBF. I'll Be Fine.

I still can't believe I'm really here. Some girls would feel this way at a concert or a fashion show, but this, *this* is my fandom. And to think, in just a few hours I will be in the same room as ZAK CANZERI. I can hardly process that.

When the speeches are over, we're ushered into the Zation room. Ethan walks toward the robotics area. Maybe he's rethinking the desk-evator concept? Hoping to make some sort of automated version? Who knows what's floating around my brother's head?

The girl from our table, Natalia, goes up to him. Hmm. What's that about? She was all over the place with her speech, talking about mandalas and staying in the moment and embracing the wholeness of the universe. I have a hard time with vague concepts like that.

I cut through the crowd to the coding/programming area, looking for Connor. I need to find out what he codes, exactly. But who's the first person I see? Marlon, of course. He's typing rapidly on his laptop, completely focused on the screen, and he's wearing noise-canceling headphones.

I turn away abruptly, then practically bump into Connor. He's tall and skinny like Ethan. "Oh, hi. I've been looking for you," I say. "Can we talk? I'd love to know what you've coded."

He shrugs, pushes up his glasses. "Not all that much. I built a website for my mom's business, and then one for my uncle. I created an app, too. Just for fun. It was pretty basic, though."

My mouth drops open. "Not all that much? Just for fun? Why didn't you say any of that in your speech? You talked about grilled cheese sandwiches. And your *dog*."

"I don't like bragging. People do it too much, you know? And I do have this *great* dog." He pulls out his phone and shows me a picture of a scruffy grayish-whitish dog. "Picasso," he says.

"Cute. Anyway, can I share my idea with you? Or did you already have a project in mind?"

"I thought I'd figure it out when I got here. I'm not a huge planner kind of person." Connor gestures to a couple of chairs by the wall. "Sure. Tell me what you got."

We sit; then I move my chair so I'm facing him. I open my briefcase, pull out my research notes. He leans back, crosses his hands behind his head, and stretches out his legs. His jeans are torn at the bottom, and one of his shoes has a hole by the toe. Okay, I'm getting his image. Casual and indifferent on the outside, brilliant tech mind on the inside.

"Let me guess," he says. "You are a huge planner kind of person?"

"Definitely. So, did you know that a main reason kids don't do well in school is because of disorganization?"

"Okay."

"I plan to create the Note to Self. It will be an all-in-one homework reminder, assignment tracker, study guide, and anti-failure guarantee. I picture a device similar to a step-tracker bracelet with a coordinating app that are both synched to your teachers' web pages. It would buzz with reminders of when things are due, always keeping you on track and organized."

"Kids would take it off," he interrupts. "Lose it."

"Not responsible kids."

"Nope. Gotta change that part."

"Excuse me, but if we work together, I would need you to code, not modify the concept."

He grins at me. "Are you always like this?"

"Like what?"

"In charge of the world."

I sit up straighter. "Yes, actually."

"Just clarifying. Go on."

"I've done a complete business plan. Figured out the financials. Brainstormed sales and marketing strategies, designed logos."

"Wow," Connor says, perhaps a little sarcastically.

I decide not to address that. "Programming isn't my

skill set. I'm an analyst. So, what do you say? Are you in?"

He unclasps his hands, sits forward, studies me with his head tilted. "Possibly."

"Possibly? Well, what's the deal breaker?"

He laughs. "The deal breaker. You're hilarious. I have to say, I admire your confidence, but if I'm in, I'm not just coding. I have an equal say in everything. It wouldn't be only your project—we'd figure it out together. I have some thoughts."

I put my notes back into my briefcase. "That's not how I see it. I have it all prepared. I'm not changing things."

"No worries. Good luck." Connor gets up and drifts toward the engineering area.

All right, back to square one. I pick up my briefcase and return to coding/programming. I find two guys who know how to code, but they inform me they're already doing a project together. Everyone else is hunched over a laptop or examining a microchip or something. Marlon hasn't moved.

I spot my brother and Natalia, still in the robotics Zation, inspecting a drone. Natalia says something and Ethan nods. Is he teaming up with her? What are they making? I tell myself not to panic, that I'll find some brilliant coder who'll love my idea *as is*.

Jet announces that we should return to the atrium. Now we have assigned tables, and when I find my name card, guess who's next to me? No, not Marlon, thankfully. Connor. What are the odds? Out of a hundred kids? He saunters over, and I realize he reminds me of Ethan, except that, obviously, Ethan has never coded anything in his life.

"Find anyone?" he asks.

"Not yet."

He takes off his glasses, cleans them on his shirt. "My offer still stands."

I shake my head.

Jet says we're going to do a Zactivity, and Imani and Maddox will demonstrate. They stand in front of the room, and Imani says, "This won't work." Maddox responds, "Yes, it will."

Then they proceed to say the same sentences over and over. This won't work; yes it will. Imani gets more insistent each time, but Maddox doesn't get mad or emotional.

Jet tells us to find a partner and do the same thing

together, and we're going to talk about why afterward. I turn to the girl on my left, but Connor, on my right, elbows me. "Partner?" he asks. I'm about to say no, but the girl has already turned to the person on her left.

"Fine."

We start saying "this won't work; yes it will." I say it to Connor first, and as I could've predicted, he's cool, calm, and unruffled. Then we switch and he starts telling me "this won't work."

I'm calm too, at first, trying to respond exactly as Maddox did, but I find myself getting annoyed. His voice is so, like, *relaxed*. Maybe it's because of our previous discussion, but all of a sudden I just burst and yell, "STOP!"

The kids at my table and several others turn around; then Jet makes his way over. I've either broken some sort of rule or failed the first Zactivity.

Jet puts his hand on the back of my chair. "Everything cool?"

Connor gives him a thumbs-up. "We're good now. We had a moment."

Jet stands there for a few seconds, then leaves. "Okay, that's enough, everyone," he says when he gets back to the front of the room. "So the reason for this Zactivity was to dramatize the *T* in TADA. Tenacity. In other words, resilience, persistence, determination." He points to the window again. "When you're out there, that's numero uno."

I bite my lip and glance at Connor. "Thanks."

"No big deal."

Jet says we can take "a breather" for a few minutes as lunch is being brought out. Two kids at my table start discussing an improved device for people with hearing loss. I glance at the girl on my left. She's scribbled *Melting Polar Ice* on a notepad. At another table I see Natalia drawing on her tablet. Ethan walks up and looks over her shoulder. Everyone's got something going already!

I clear my throat. "Connor?"

He shoots me a grin. "What now, Person in Charge? You changed your mind?"

"Um, well, yes. I have, actually."

"Good, because I like your idea and I didn't really have anything all that solid. But we're partners on this, right? Fifty-fifty."

"Yes. I—I'm open to your thoughts."

He reaches out to shake my hand. "Then it's a deal."

I shake firmly. A server places a plate of pasta in front of me, and I spread my napkin on my lap. I had to agree; I need him. I'll just have to assess how that fifty-fifty arrangement goes.

After lunch we get a fifteen-minute break. I grab my phone and immediately text Zoe. She texted me hours ago, but I couldn't reply.

I met this guy Connor who likes the NTS idea and he codes!

She responds immediately. That's great!

He created two websites and an app!

Yay! Have you met Z?

Not yet. This afternoon.

Sad-face emoji. I wish I was there.

Me too. It's completely amazing. I don't want to make her feel worse, so I ask, How's everything there?

Not so good. I forgot how my aunt talks ALL the time like Hannah. She even yells to us while she's in the bathroom. And all they do is watch football.

So annoying.

How's Ethan?

Haven't talked to him since we got here. I think he's working with this girl Natalia.

Zoe doesn't answer.

Don't worry, I say.

Is she cute?

She's weird. Like, all spiritual. Do you know what a mandala is?

Yes.

That was her project that got her into the camp. Something with mandalas and autism.

Are they hanging out a lot?

I don't know. But don't worry, okay?

She responds a minute later: I always worry.

CHAPTER SIXTEEN

Cleared for Takeoff

ETHAN

Something weird about dreams. They vanish the instant you wake up, but then you remember something later, usually at the strangest moment. I don't get why that happens.

Anyway, while I was listening to everyone's speeches, Mrs. Slovenko popped into my mind. I don't have music until next quarter, but everyone loves her. She turns everything into a song, I hear, even when she's taking attendance.

I was thinking about how I saw her adjusting the music stand on the last day of school before winter break; then I remembered how she was doing that in my mixed-up dream. Next thing it was like I was hit with a Z lightning bolt. I can't explain it, but the idea for the new and improved desk-evator was just THERE. In a flash I knew what it looked like and how it would work.

I grabbed my gold pencil, flipped over a piece of paper from my Zacket, and started sketching. Natalia glanced over. "What's that?" she whispered.

"A really cool standing desk. For school."

She redid a braid and watched me draw.

Later, when we were at the robotics Zation, I told her the whole story: Invention Day, the failed desk-evator, Ethan Squiggle Disease, even my dream. I described my new idea and—get this—she asked if she could work with me!

"Dreams are a window to our creativity," she said. "My brother often cries when he dreams. They are more powerful than we realize."

"Yeah, sure," I answered. I was just ecstatic that someone liked what I'd come up with.

We were looking at the drone when I remembered something else. I only saw Mrs. Slovenko adjusting the music stand because I stopped to read Wesley's flyer. You have to admit the timing of that is a little freaky.

Did Wesley unintentionally help me again? Who knows. Doesn't matter, I guess. I'm cleared for takeoff!

During the break I pull out my phone and text Brian. I got it!

What?

The way to make it new and improved!

Sweet. What is it?

I'm calling it DESK ON A STICK.

He doesn't reply.

Like a music stand! The desk part slides up and down a long post, and there's a stool that unfolds when you want to sit. It's an all-in-one unit, not just on a desktop. And it's on WHEELS!

Well, I have to say, things on a stick are awesome. Popsicles, lollipops, chicken satay.

Right! This is it! It appeared in a vision or something!! I'm going nuts with exclamation points.

Brian sends me an eye-roll emoji. Don't get all deep on me, Marcus.

Sorry, but true. And this girl Natalia likes my idea. We're teaming up. She thinks it should have holders for supplies and stuff.

See, just as I predicted, you're getting sucked into Canzeri world.

It is a little weird here. They change words to start with Z, like Zation instead of station. Everything's black and gold. And the Z Team people are kinda robotic.

Sounds like a cult.

What do you know about cults?

You hear things. Anyway, wanna know what I've been doing? I helped my dad sweep pine needles from under the tree. I listened to Gram snore. I went to Target with my mom for the after-Christmas sale. I broke the blender. That was fun.

How'd you do that?

In my defense, it was a really old blender. I was making a smoothie, but the blender sounded like an injured animal. I took off the lid and it turned into a geyser. Fruit shot up at the ceiling. The motor blew.

Awesome.

No. Not awesome. I'm banned from the kitchen.

Nice. I gotta go. They're blinking the lights.

Spooky.

Don't blow anything else up.

Don't join a cult.

I go back to the table I was sitting at in the morning. Natalia's already there. She pats the seat of the chair next to her, then whispers, "Z is about to make his entrance."

Just then, the lights go out.

ETHAN

In the middle of the atrium, there's a puff of smoke. Gold laser lights rocket around the room—in the shape of *Z*s—and loud music starts playing. When the smoke fades, this guy is standing there. Really tall, thin, dark hair, sunglasses. Black pants and a black shirt, with hands casually in his pants pockets.

Jet grabs the microphone and motions to Imani. The music stops. "The man before us needs no introduction," Jet says, and everyone claps crazily. I see Erin, sitting next to Connor. Her eyes are popping out of her head, and her mouth is open a mile wide.

Z takes the microphone but can't say a word for several minutes because of the cheering and applause. Finally the room quiets down, and Z says in a low voice, "How ya doin', all you Z people?"

Kids start going nuts again; then Z holds up his palm and it gets silent. He presses his hand to his heart. "I'm genuinely touched by your welcome. But *I* should be cheering for *you*." He sweeps an arm, like he's a conductor. "You, every one of you in this room, are the people who will shape the world of the future. A world we have just barely begun to imagine. I have no doubt you will do amazing work here. To innovate is not only to invent and create; it is to revolutionize. Go. Do. Be."

He lifts his arm into the air and draws an invisible *Z* with one finger; then the lights go out and the puff of smoke appears again. When it fades and the lights are back on, Z is gone.

Kids start murmuring and whispering. Erin has her head on the table she's sitting at, like she passed out or something. Natalia's staring at the spot where Z stood. "Wow. Where did he go? Do you think there was a trapdoor?"

"Maybe," I say, craning my neck. "I don't see one."

"Magicians are so intriguing," she says. "I always try to figure out how they do their tricks. They make it look so real, but you know there's always a catch."

Jet announces it's time to start figuring out our projects and decide if we're working with others or alone. We can go back to the Zations anytime, he says, and consult with the Z Team. "And remember, think Z!"

Natalia pulls out her tablet. "Should we get started?" I nod, still watching the last bits of smoke disappear. Where *did* he go?

"First," she says, "I think we need to address the engineering component. How's the standing desk going to work? What do we use to build it? How will we attach the stool?"

I can't help but laugh.

"What's wrong?"

"Nothing. Nothing at all." I remember me and Brian in my basement, trying to make the desk-evator out of ridiculous materials that didn't even make sense. So this is what it's like to work with someone who knows what they're doing.

I grab my rough sketch. "Okay. Let's talk engineering."

ERIN

Connor and I stay in the atrium. We power up our laptops, and I spread my notes across the table. I see Ethan and Natalia go into the Zation room.

Connor scratches his chin. "I'm not diggin' the bracelet device idea."

"Yes, you said that." I clasp my hands tightly in my lap. "All right, I'm willing to listen."

"I'm thinking an app is the best way to go, but truthfully, apps are getting old. And there's too many. I think we need to be more innovative. Come up with something unique."

"Like what?"

"I'm not sure. We need to kick that around a little." Connor gestures to my notes. "Before we jump right into marketing and sales."

"Well, what do kids have with them all the time besides their phones? Maybe we could create a pencil with a built-in chip? Or how about an ID card of some sort?"

"I like it, but kids could lose those, too."

"You have something about kids losing things."

"Yeah, happens a lot. I'm a big loser." He laughs. "Of things."

I smile. "So, something kids couldn't lose."

He stands, runs a hand over his cropped, curly hair.

"I like the idea of something that synchs with teachers' web pages. And I like the reminder aspect to keep kids on track with homework and projects. But it has to be something kids would want to use, that would maybe even be fun."

"Yes."

He sits down. "What about an Apple Watch kind of thing? Still losable, but cooler."

"How is that different from a bracelet? And wouldn't it be more expensive to produce?" I drum my nails on the table as Connor reaches into his backpack, pulls out a small spiral notebook, and starts leafing through it.

"What's that?" I ask.

He shrugs. "My assignments. Talking about all this made me remember I need to get a book I'm supposed to read over break."

"You still use an assignment notebook? So do I. Actually, lots of kids do." I push a stray frizzy hair off my forehead. "Wait . . ." I clasp my hands excitedly. "WAIT!"

He looks up.

"IDEA! What about some type of little device that

would clip onto an assignment notebook? Like a virtual assistant?"

He tilts his head. "Hmm. But it has to be entertaining, maybe even addicting. What about something like a Giga Pet?"

"What's a Giga Pet?"

"It was this fad in the nineties. I have one. I love vintage electronic stuff. They were these small digital devices on a key chain that kids hung from their backpacks. You took care of a computerized dog or cat."

Connor finds a picture of a Giga Pet on his phone and shows me. "Pretty great, until you forgot to feed it and the thing died on you. I wouldn't have put that in the program. We could come up with something hilarious, like a talking banana."

I nod, the possibilities zooming around in my head. "I don't know about the banana, but I think we've got an idea."

Connor points to my stack of papers. "No insult, but we can do better than Note to Self. We need something catchier."

"I—I agree."

"Good." He pulls his laptop closer. "Let me do a little scouting around. See how I could potentially set this up. You wanna start brainstorming different names? And revise some of the strategies?"

"All right. I can do that."

He wakes up his laptop. A picture of his dog is the background. Connor sees me looking and says, "He's a mutt. We rescued him."

"Oh. Why Picasso?"

"When we got him, we thought his face looked like the Picasso sculpture in downtown Chicago. You ever see it?"

"Yeah. We went to the city for a play. The sculpture's a little strange. What's it supposed to be?"

"Whatever you think. That's the beauty of it."

"I prefer art that's more specific, not something you have to try to figure out."

He laughs and starts typing. I mean, I do. Why was that funny? I reorganize my papers and push up the lead on my pencil. Then I get to work.

After I dig in a bit, I start to feel excited about the new idea, and I'm making definite progress revising my plan. Connor seems to be immersed in whatever he's doing. Okay, yes, I admit, he had some good thoughts. Jet announces a fifteen-minute break, and we decide to compare notes afterward.

I quickly head to the bathroom, realizing I haven't gone all day. When I'm in a stall, I hear two girls come in and start talking. It's impossible not to eavesdrop when you're in this situation.

One says, "Did you hear about that guy who's supposedly working on some kind of tiny voice-activated personal assistant?"

The other one says, "No. What's the scoop?"

"I guess it, like, attaches to your ear or your shirt and does anything you need."

"Like Siri?"

"Better. Like your own little guide to the universe."

They could be talking about anyone, right? They're going to think I'm insane, but I call out, "Excuse me, but what's the guy's name? Do you know?"

There's silence for a second; then one of the girls says, "I don't remember."

Then the other one goes, "It was the guy who said in

his speech that he was going to win. And if what people are saying is true, he probably will."

"Thank you," I choke out.

Not anyone. Him. Of course. Why would it be any other way?

CHAPTER EIGHTEEN

Day One, Done

ETHAN

I'm on my way to the car when I realize I forgot my Zacket. I run back inside Gotham City. Everyone's gone. I spot it right away on the table I was sitting at. It's the only one in the place. I grab it and head to the door.

When I'm about to push it open, I hear a phone ringing, then someone whispering in a panicky-sounding voice, "Don't answer it! I haven't slept in weeks. They can wait another day!"

I turn and see Z and Maddox standing halfway down a darkened hallway. Z's back is to me, but it's for sure him. No wonder the guy never takes off his sunglasses if he hasn't slept in weeks. Maddox spots me and puts a hand on Z's arm. He turns and they both wave. "Have a great night," Maddox calls.

"Thanks." I rush out to the car. What was that all about?

Erin's already in the backseat when I get there, her head turned toward the window.

"Hey," Dad says to me. "How'd it go?"

I slide in, buckle. "Pretty good, actually. I found someone to work with, and I got a great idea for how to make the desk-evator way better!"

Dad pulls away from the curb. "Excellent."

"Did Erin tell you how Zak Canzeri made this big entrance with smoke and laser lights, then disappeared?"

"No." Dad glances in the rearview mirror. "Your sister's been unusually quiet."

Erin kicks off Mom's shoes, then rubs her ankle. I catch a whiff of smelly feet. Why'd she wear those? I'm sure they made her feet sweat. And stink.

Awkward silence for a few seconds. Then I go, "Okay, what's wrong?"

"Nothing." She straightens her briefcase on her lap.

When Erin says nothing's wrong, something always is.

"So . . . how's your project going? You're working with Connor, right?"

All of a sudden, words just start pouring out of her at rapid speed.

"I had a great idea too. No, an amazing one! I've been working on it for *weeks*. Note to Self, but we're changing the name. Which is fine. A device to keep kids on track in school and assure their success. Connor came up with the Giga Pet aspect and it's good. He's super smart, in this casual, ripped-blue-jeans kind of way." She hiccups loudly. "Anyway, we were going along nicely and I was getting excited, really feeling it, you know, and then I heard these girls in the bathroom talking. My virtual assistant is just for school, but his is for everything, apparently! I mean, how is that even possible?"

As I said.

She hiccups again. "And if what I overheard is true, and I don't doubt that it is, then my idea isn't going to cut it, Ethan. It's just not BIG ENOUGH, do you understand?"

"Uh . . . this has to do with Romanov?"

She sighs. "Who else would I be talking about?"

"Some girls in the bathroom?" Dad pipes in. "It's probably just gossip. A rumor."

"I don't think so." She opens the window, sucks in some air. "I can't let him get to me. Not again. What I have to do is figure out how to make my device bigger, better, flashier. Actually, now that I'm thinking about it, this is good. I'm lucky I found this out early in the game. I'll talk to Connor first thing tomorrow."

"Glad I could assist," I say.

Erin closes the window, points to my wrist. "What is that?"

"An energy band."

"Let me guess. Natalia?"

"Uh-huh. She says it'll help my productivity and creativity."

"It's just a rubber bracelet."

"Who knows? I need all the help I can get with my desk on a stick."

"Wait, what?"

I grin. "That's what we're calling the new and improved desk-evator. It's a whole new concept. Freestanding, on wheels, with a stool that pops out. It can be moved any-where in a classroom. How cool is that? We started design-ing the prototype today."

Erin tilts her head. "Well, that's certainly better than what you had before."

"Natalia's really good at engineering stuff. And she's totally on board." I elbow Erin. "Did you hear that? I just used a cool business term. On board."

"I'm happy you're finally stepping up and learning the terminology."

"CEO, big picture, reach out, circle back." I bob my head. "I got this."

"Wonderful." She rubs her ankle again.

"Maybe you shouldn't wear those shoes tomorrow?"

"No, they're fine. I need to look professional." She pulls a pencil and pad of paper from her briefcase and starts crossing things out and scribbling notes.

When we get home, Mom wants to hear every detail. Erin gives her what she calls the 360-degree view, describing everything except the bathroom encoun-ter. "The bottom line is that it was truly amazing. I can barely process it all."

I've been eating bagel chips this whole time. Sesame, the best kind.

Mom glances at me. "Dinner in a few. Don't fill up on chips."

"I barely had anything to eat there," I protest. "They need to put out more snacks."

"Didn't you see the protein bars on the tables?" Erin asks.

"Yeah, I tried one. It was horrible. It tasted like tree bark or something."

"So, what was Zak Canzeri like?" Mom asks.

"We only saw him for about two minutes," I answer. "Then he vanished in a puff of smoke."

"Really?" Mom says. "That seems odd."

"It's all part of his image," Erin says. "Anyway, tomorrow we're supposed to have a guest speaker and some surprise Zactivities."

"Zactivities?" Dad repeats.

"It's a branding thing. Zackets, Zations, Zactivities," Erin explains.

Mom raises her eyebrows. "Clever."

Erin hasn't said anything about the Romanov issue, and I'm certainly not bringing it up.

We sit down for dinner. She heaps some mashed potatoes on her plate, then announces, "I have a lot of work to do tonight, so if you all wouldn't mind keeping the noise level down, I have to concentrate."

"Sure," Dad says.

"Of course," Mom agrees.

Erin looks at me. "The ball?"

"Fine, I won't hit it against the wall."

"Thank you again for letting me go," Erin says to Mom and Dad. "It's everything I expected, and so much more. I can hardly wait for tomorrow."

"Yeah," I say. "Me too."

It is pretty much what I expected. Genius World, with me, the visitor from Duct Tape Land. But I made it through day number one, didn't I? And I found someone who likes my idea! Natalia says sitting is "against the flow of nature." She says the human body isn't made to be in a sitting position for hours at a time. How's that, huh?

I can hardly wait for tomorrow too. I think my desk on a stick is really gonna fly. Did you catch that? Fly, as in soar. As in the sky's the limit. As in I'm not an idiot anymore.

CHAPTER NINETEEN

An Ant and an Aunt

ERIN

I read and research until I'm bleary-eyed. When Zoe's face pops up on my phone to FaceTime, I answer immediately.

"I'm so happy you called!" I shout when she comes into focus. "I have so much to tell you!"

I report on all the events at camp, from the speeches to the Zations to Z's appearance to working with Connor.

"That all sounds great," Zoe says.

I frown. "Except, *Marlon*."

"What happened?"

"I overheard these girls say he's designing some kind of voice-activated personal assistant that attaches to your ear or something."

"Okay . . ."

"That's huge, Zoe. My project is just to help kids do

better in school. His is to . . . I don't even know, but it'll make mine look basic. Like a simplified version."

"Erin. Don't think about what he's doing. Focus on what you're doing."

"You're right, of course, but it's hard. He just gets under my skin. And the kids at the camp, they're all brilliant. Their projects are amazing. I don't know if mine—"

The door behind Zoe opens, and I see her mom. She tells Zoe it's late and she's going to bed. After she leaves, Zoe turns back to the screen, shaking her head.

"How's it going there?" I ask. "And where are you, by the way? I see food in the background."

"I'm in their walk-in pantry. It was the only private place I could find. They have a lot of junk food. My cousins never stop eating. As for how it's going, well, let's see. Marci's been lecturing my mom about picking herself up and not wallowing in self-pity, and she keeps criticizing my dad. Especially now, with the baby."

I almost drop my phone as Zoe covers her mouth. "What baby?" I shout.

"I—I've been meaning to tell you, but with the camp and us leaving and everything . . ."

"Who's having a baby?"

"My dad. I mean, Dara. They're . . . getting married."

"Oh my God! When did all this happen?"

"A few weeks ago. Erin, I'm sorry. I couldn't talk about it. . . ." Zoe's eyes brim with tears.

"It's okay. Are you all right?"

She shrugs. "Not really. I've been thinking about dropping the Kramer from my name now. A hyphenated last name is pretty ridiculous when your parents are divorced and your dad lives in another country and is having a kid with someone else, don't you think?"

"Are you saying you'd legally change it?"

"Yes. Zoe Feld. How does it sound?"

"Good. It sounds good. If that's what you want."

We're quiet for a second. Zoe wipes her eyes, then leans back against a row of cereal boxes on a shelf. "In other news, a woodpecker has been living in our mailbox. Mom wants to call an animal service when we get back to have it removed. I keep begging her not to."

I laugh. "So, we've got a baby on the way and a woodpecker in the mailbox. Anything else you want to tell me?"

"Yeah . . ." She sniffles. "I don't know what's happening

with Ethan, either. The last day before break, I wished him good luck at camp, and he barely answered me."

"He always barely answers."

"Has he said anything to you? About me?"

"No, but he wouldn't," I reply. "Listen, he's not all that great, you know. When he doesn't have any clean clothes, he takes stuff out of the dirty pile and wears them. His shirts have, like, food stains. How gross is that?"

"I think that's kind of sweet."

"How can it be sweet? It's smelly. And icky."

Zoe cry-laughs.

"And he's so oblivious all the time. He loses everything and never knows what's going on."

"I love that about him." She looks down. "Does he like that girl? Natalia?"

"I don't know. They're just doing a project together, as far as I know. Do you want me to ask him?"

She doesn't answer.

"I'll see what I can find out, without asking him."

"Thanks."

"No problem."

"And, Erin, it'll be all right. The thing with Marlon."

"How do you know?"

"I know because you'll make it all right. You always do."

ZOE

I open the pantry door and peek out. The kitchen's dark. The only sound I hear is Hannah's giggling in the guest room. There's a girl across the street who's exactly Hannah's age, and they made friends in, like, five minutes. She's sleeping over. Their giggling gets louder, and I hear Aunt Marci go, "Shh! That's enough now, girls!"

More giggling, then it gets quiet. My sister reminds me of this wobbly penguin toy I had when I was little. You'd push it down and it would spring back up every time. Major life stuff happens and Hannah bounces right back. I don't know how a person can be like that.

I tiptoe over to the sink and open the cabinet underneath, then take out the garbage can. Quietly and quickly, I find every single recyclable item and rinse them all. Then I get a paper bag from the pantry, put everything inside, and go out the front door, closing it behind me softly but leaving it unlocked.

Aunt Marci's neighbors keep their recycling bin on

the side of their house. I noticed that the day we arrived. In the few days we've been here, I've saved numerous cans, containers, papers, and boxes from going to a landfill. I know it's not much, but every little bit helps, right?

I go back inside, and I'm about to switch off the light in the pantry when I spot an ant, carrying a crumb, making its way across the tile floor. The crumb must be ten times its weight, probably more. I watch it steadily move toward a corner, struggling with the crumb, but at the same time never stopping.

Most people don't know that ants are amazing insects. They're incredibly strong, organized, and efficient, and they're natural problem solvers. Humans could learn a lot from them.

I didn't realize that ants could survive in the cold months, though. Where is the colony? Under the floor? The ant disappears into a crack. Maybe so. Wherever they are, they're going to have a good meal tonight. For some reason, that makes me feel the tiniest bit better.

CHAPTER TWENTY

Commotion

ERIN

The second day of camp begins with a guest speaker from a start-up (fascinating), then a Zactivity on marketing (a lot of which I know already), a fifteen-minute yoga/meditation break (Natalia looks thrilled), and finally time to work on our projects.

Connor brought in a Giga Pet, and we've been analyzing it and working on the design for our device. Connor's been investigating the coding side of things, and TBH, I have no idea what he's doing. Thankfully, he seems to have it under control. I've been revising the business plan and trying to come up with a name *and* a way to make it more spectacular. Nothing yet, but I'll keep you posted.

I've been watching my brother, too. As far as I can tell, he and Natalia are only doing the project together.

I'm not picking up any romantic signals or anything. Good news to report to Zoe later.

They seem to be zooming right along with their desk-on-a-stick idea, tinkering with some metal pieces and hammering sections together. I can't tell how it's supposed to work, but it seems a lot better than what he created with Brian.

Jet announces that lunch is in ten minutes and we should "reach a closing point." I slide my notepad into my briefcase and place it under the table. A hushed murmur spreads through the atrium, and when I look up, Z is standing at the front of the room.

My heart rate quickens. "Oh my God. Look. Z's here."

"I see," Connor says, still tapping on his keyboard.

Z glides over to a table, starts talking to some kids.

I stand, then sit, then stand again. "What if he comes over here? It looks like he's asking those kids about their project. I'm not ready. We're not ready, Connor. We're not at the point where we can show this to him."

He runs a hand over his hair. "Take it easy. We can show him what we have so far if he asks. I'm sure that's all right. No one's done yet."

Jet holds the microphone close to his mouth. "As you can see, Z is in the house."

Everyone applauds. Jet puts up a hand and waits until everyone quiets down. "Please go ahead and grab some chow. While you're eating, Z will be visiting your tables to check in. Do not come to him, people. He will come to you. Got it? Good. And absolutely no selfies. Z doesn't do them. Ever."

People go over to the food table and get in line, and I follow along. My legs feel wooden, but at the same time it's like I'm floating. When I'm closer to Z, I get a whiff of the spicy cologne he must be wearing, and I don't know how, but a little squeaky "Hi" escapes from my mouth.

Z turns and LOOKS AT ME. Then he nods—almost imperceptibly—and smiles. He has the whitest, shiniest teeth I've ever seen.

My eyes get wide, and I freeze, right on the spot. Suddenly someone bumps into me, hard, and I lose my balance. As I flail my arms, trying to stay upright but failing miserably, I have a fleeting thought—why did I have to wear Mom's heels?—then my arm knocks into a plate of food, and a second later I hit the floor, land flat on my back, and feel something wet and slimy on my leg.

Why, why, why?

I sit up, a little dizzy, and see a glop of hummus on my leg. Oh God, no! Did Z witness this whole unfortunate episode? I crane my neck but can't even see him anymore, because Maddox, Asher, and Imani surround me like an emergency-response team. Imani offers me a black cloth napkin, Asher picks up the overturned plate, and Maddox starts wiping the floor.

"No worries," she says. "We're used to people freaking out in Z's presence. Happens all the time."

Marlon. It was Marlon who bumped into me. I glare at him. "Did you not see me standing there?"

"You were not standing. You were walking," he answers calmly, almost robotically, then just leaves. I leap to my feet and brush off my skirt, then wipe the hummus with the napkin.

"All back to normal," Asher says, dumping the plate into a trash can. There's no trace of anything on the floor. Like it never happened. And where did Z go? I don't see him anywhere.

Ethan comes over; a second later Connor's there

too. "Uh, are you okay?" Ethan asks. He looks at my leg. "You've still got some hummus by your knee—"

"Yes, thank you very much." I point at Connor. "Do not, I repeat, *do not* tell me to take it easy."

He puts up his hands. "Wasn't gonna."

I clean off the last of the hummus as Natalia approaches me and offers her tablet. "Do you want to try a mandala? They're very calming."

"Thanks, but those kinds of things don't work on me."

"I'm pretty good at reading moods. It'll help, I promise—"

"Okay, everyone, I appreciate your concern, but I'm fine. No bruises, no scrapes." I square my shoulders, straighten my sweater. "Moving forward."

ETHAN

Erin marches off to the bathroom a little unsteadily. Natalia watches her, then says, "She's not fine. If there's anyone in need of a mandala, it's your sister." She hurries after Erin.

"That's not going to go well," I say.

Connor laughs. "Yeah, I can definitely see that."

I look around. "Where's Z? I thought he was checking people's projects."

Connor shrugs. "Who knows?" He lowers his voice. "The camp's named after him, but isn't it odd that he's never here?"

"Well, he's an important guy, right?"

"I know, but I don't dig that. If you're going to make this whole big deal about giving your time to kids and the future, then *do* it."

"Good point."

He gestures, and I see Erin coming out of the bathroom with Natalia next to her, holding out an energy band. Erin's not taking it.

"Oh boy," I say, then turn to Connor. "You're okay working with my sister? She's a little . . . intense."

"Really?" He grins. "I hadn't noticed."

"Romanov makes her crazy. He won Invention Day at our school last year, and she wants to get back at him or something. Ruin his life, you know."

"Seems like you guys are complete opposites."

"Yeah, we are."

"I just have a stepbrother, and he lives in Seattle, so

I don't see him very often. It's kind of amusing to watch you two go at it."

"'Amusing' wouldn't be the word I'd pick, but okay. Anyway, I know she's glad you're doing the coding and everything."

He shoves his hands into his jean pockets. "Actually, if you want to know the truth, I'm not even supposed to be here."

"What do you mean? Weren't you nominated?"

"Nope, not at first."

"How'd you get in, then?"

"Simple. The first three people couldn't go."

"Wait, seriously?"

"Yep. There are a couple of brainiacs at my school who should've been here instead of me. I just kinda fool around with this stuff for fun. I'm not serious about it. These guys are. They couldn't get out of prior commitments."

I wonder why Gilardi didn't nominate other kids when Zoe and Brian couldn't go. Maybe it was too late, or the camp was full?

"But you came anyway?" I ask.

"My parents made me. They didn't want me to pass

up the opportunity. They were like, 'maybe things happen for a reason' and all that junk. They want me to work at some big tech company someday. But who wants to spend their life as a programmer? Staring at a screen for eight hours every day? I can't think of anything I'd want to do less."

"What do you want to do?"

"Either be a vet or a chef. Dogs and food. Now we're talking."

"That's cool. I love food."

"Yeah." He smiles. "Me too."

M.R.

I need my book. I need my armor. I should've brought it. Why didn't I bring it?

Erin Marcus was *walking*. How could I have known she would stop right in front of me? Was that a nuance? Social cue? Why are they so difficult to detect? I will never learn how.

I return to my table and put on my headphones. The noise in the room grows faint. *Continue, continue. Put it out of your mind. Stop shaking.*

I open my laptop cover, place my fingertips on the keyboard, then feel a tap on my shoulder. I look up. It is Maddox. She makes a motion for me to take off the headphones, and I remove them.

"Hey, are you okay? Just wanted to check."

"I am not hurt."

She tilts her head, studies me for a brief moment. "That's good. But, like, otherwise, I mean?"

I don't know how to answer that question. I stare at her. She has brown eyes. The color of 60-percent cacao.

Maddox waves her hand. "I have a lot of dumb accidents, so don't be embarrassed or anything. I like to walk and read at the same time, and that's a dangerous endeavor. Once, I fell off a curb and sprained my ankle. No joke."

"I see."

"And there was another time I walked into a stop sign. Kinda funny, don't you think? *Stop*, right? Duh."

I blink.

"So, anyway, you're fine?" she asks.

I nod and reach for my headphones.

"You have any questions?"

"No."

She sweeps a fist in the air. "Okay, then, onward!"

Maddox walks away, and I turn to my screen.

Interesting observation: 60-percent cacao is Mom's favorite type of chocolate.

CHAPTER TWENTY-ONE

Moving Toward the Future

ERIN

When we arrive on the third day, Jet tells us to keep our coats on. We're going on a hike, he says, on a nature trail that winds around the campus. But it's not a regular hike. We are required to (1) not talk and (2) wear snowshoes. So that's why they told us to bring boots today.

Jet explains that from past experience they know this is the point in the camp where kids start running into problems with their projects, and silently navigating a hiking trail with the snowshoes will help us work through any knots or trouble spots.

"At the summer camps we wear flippers," he says, zipping up a shiny black ski jacket. "This is a definite challenge, and you'll be frustrated, but trust us."

We get our snowshoes, and Imani demonstrates how to strap them on. People start putting them on, but I decide to wait until I get out to the trail. Which I quickly learn is a big mistake. Everyone clomps silently ahead in the snow, but I'm still fastening mine, and my fingers get icy cold in a few minutes.

I finally get them on and take a few unsteady steps. If you've never tried to walk in a pair of snowshoes, let me just say it's like having tennis rackets strapped to your feet. And honestly, I don't know who would ever want to do that. There must be a reason these were invented, but I can't figure it out.

Connor's at the end of the group, looking back at me. By doing some sort of awkward clomp-step-hop, I catch up to him. His glasses are foggy, and he doesn't look happy either. We start walking, but I keep getting my snowshoe caught on his and almost trip both of us a couple of times. The rest of the kids and the Z Team are way ahead.

Connor picks up a long, thin branch and hands it to me, motioning that I should use it as a pole. I mouth, "Thanks." It's probably against the rules, but I use it anyway, poking it in the snow as I try to walk.

A few minutes later we reach the group, standing and

drinking from their water bottles. They're all looking at us. Silently. Natalia, next to Ethan, places her palms together and nods at me. I have no idea what she's trying to say.

Jet points, and everyone falls into a line, then starts moving again. I take a quick drink from my water bottle. Marlon's directly in front of me now.

His steps are even and controlled, like he's worn snowshoes all his life. With each step he lifts his knee and puts his foot down perfectly flat on the ground. I start thinking about how I fell in front of everyone and feel embarrassed all over again. I only fell because he crashed into me. I can't help but wonder, did he do it on purpose? Would he really do something that mean? I don't know, but I keep watching him walk steadily . . . not stumbling once. . . . Then I really trip and lose hold of the stick, and it happens.

I ERUPT.

I break the no-talking rule.

"Stop acting like you're better than everyone else!" I yell. "Your robotic hand didn't even place at Invention Day! You were disqualified, remember?"

Connor whispers, "Erin," but I brush a hand at him.

"You don't know what happened, okay? You don't know what he said to me."

Marlon's face is blank. He crosses his arms, but weirdly, like he's hugging himself. *He* doesn't break the no-talking rule.

Jet moves toward us with his finger across his lips; then Z appears out of nowhere, through a clump of trees. He's not wearing snowshoes. He's not even wearing a jacket. He strolls casually in between Marlon and me, separating us with his silent coolness. Everyone is quietly watching: two hundred blinking eyes.

"People," he says, looking around. "The vibe I'm getting . . . it isn't very Z." He's wearing dark sunglasses like usual, even though the sky is gray, not even one peek of sun.

I bite my lip. "I'm so sorry." Is he going to ask me to leave the camp? "I—I . . . It won't happen again."

Marlon says nothing.

Z holds his arms out. "We are all innovators. We are all techpreneurs. We work together. We support each other. We champion each other."

"Right." I sniffle. "TADA," I choke out.

Marlon still says nothing.

Z clasps his hands. No gloves, either. Isn't he cold? "Tensions are high, my friends. We must stay focused, not let our fears get the best of us. Comparison," he says, "is the thief of joy. Words of wisdom from my comrade Theodore Roosevelt."

I bob my head. "Yes."

"All right. Let's put this behind us." Z gestures to the snowy path. "The only way to move is toward the future. Go. Do. Be." Z waits for us to start, then joins the back of the group as we clomp ahead in the snowshoes, finally, thankfully, circling back to the building.

Connor comes up to me when we're inside. "Erin, listen. I think you have Marlon all wrong. It's not about you."

"What are you talking about?" I whisper.

"I know guys like that. I go to a prep school, okay? Think about it. The only one Marlon is battling against . . . is himself."

I shake my head. "That's not how it is. Don't try to analyze this. You don't know him."

"I don't have to. I can tell." Connor takes off his

snowshoes and places them on the pile by the front door.

I see Marlon walking stiffly toward the table he always sits at. In a second he's got his headphones on and his laptop open. The chairs on either side of him are empty. His fingers are poised above the keyboard, but he's not typing; he's just staring at the screen like he's in a trance.

Connor nudges me. "You plan to keep those on all day? Getting attached to them?" He points to my snowshoes.

I unstrap both, add them to the pile. I keep watching Marlon as we head toward our table. He blows his nose with a tissue; then a minute later he starts typing furiously. Connor's wrong. Marlon just wants to win, like he announced to everyone. And that kind of person doesn't care who gets in his way.

ETHAN

Well, that was crazy. I thought the snowshoe hike was one of the best things we've done here, but Erin obviously didn't agree. I consider asking her if she's okay, but knowing my sister, that'll make it worse. Whatever "it" is. While I get it's something to do with Marlon, the details are always much more involved than I even imagine.

Z tells us to continue moving "toward the future," then turns down a hallway. The same one he was in with Maddox that first day, when I overheard him. He stops and pulls out his phone. I can't hear what he's saying, but his voice sounds completely different from when he was talking to us on the trail. Not so smooth and calm. More like, I don't know, nervous. Suddenly he shouts, "There's no problem!" and slips into a room. The door shuts with a loud click.

I glance over my shoulder. No one's near me. No kids, none of the Z Team people. We're on a short break, and everyone's in the atrium. I catch Z's voice, shouting again. "I'm on top of it!"

Before I change my mind, I walk casually down the hallway, hands in my jean pockets. I'm right by the room Z went into when I hear, "Excuse me, what are you doing?"

I jump about a foot in the air. It's Imani, frowning, arms crossed, her eyes like two intense laser beams.

"Oh, my bad, I, uh, got lost."

"You shouldn't be in this hallway. No one is allowed here. It's off-limits."

"Right. I—I . . . there was a line at the bathroom. I was looking for another one."

Her mouth is a tight, straight line. "Please return to the atrium immediately."

I hurry away, glancing back at her. She's watching me. That was weird. Very weird. What's going on? Why is that hallway off-limits?

As I sit down next to Natalia, Imani comes into the atrium. She goes up to Asher and whispers something. They both scan the room, stopping their gazes to rest on me for a brief second. Then they assume their usual poker faces.

Okay, that was even weirder. And suddenly I get this shivery little feeling that things in Z land aren't exactly as they appear to be.

ZOE

A lot of people text in all caps and you don't always know why, but with Erin it's pretty clear. DISTRESS.

I get this all-cap text from her: I LOST IT.

I'm completely confused. You lost what?

MY COOL. I YELLED AT MARLON ON THE HIKING TRAIL. WE WEREN'T SUPPOSED TO TALK. DISASTER WITH A CAPITAL D.

Oh, Erin!

I know. I have to go. We're starting up again. Connor and I need to build a model, and fast. We're so behind.

I'll be home tonight. I'll come over. Whatever happened, we'll fix it. I'll help you! I text her some smileys and hearts, but she doesn't respond.

I zip my duffel bag and bring it to the front door. We're just about to get on the road. Hannah hugs her new friend, and both of them cry like they've known each other for years. Mom hugs Aunt Marci. I don't feel like hugging anyone.

Marci shakes a finger at Mom. "Now, you listen to all that advice I gave you."

Mom nods, then reaches for our bags.

"Can I help?" I ask.

She smiles at me. "I got it."

Mom slings a bag over each shoulder and picks up the third, then walks out and loads them into the trunk.

She reminds me of the ant with the crumb on its back. Even if she gets tired a lot, she's still pretty strong. She keeps going.

"Good-bye, girls," Aunt Marci says to me and Hannah. "Have a safe trip." Hannah runs out to the car, but I turn to Marci. I have to say what's on my mind, and fast, without her interrupting.

"You might not think so, but recycling is important. It's little, but big at the same time." I point to a window by the kitchen sink. "I found your recycling bin in the garage and put it right under that window. All you have to do is open it, drop in an item, then roll it out to the curb once a week. Pickup is on Monday. I checked the website."

Marci stares down at me—surprised, mad, I don't know. She's quiet for once.

"And one other thing." My voice catches. "Even with everything that happened, my dad's not a bad person."

I don't wait for a reply or a comment or anything. I walk right out into the bright sun, feel the beautiful cold air against my skin, then get into the car. Hannah sniffles, wipes her eyes, and clamps on her headphones.

Mom turns up the heat, and I buckle my seat belt.

"It's nice to be going home," she says.

I draw a heart on the frosty window. "It is."

Mom backs out of the driveway as Marci closes the front door. A few minutes later we're on the highway. Hannah starts singing. Loudly, of course.

Mom and I smile at each other; then she shrugs and looks straight out at the road ahead. I do the same.

CHAPTER TWENTY-TWO

Brian-storm

ETHAN

That night Brian comes over, and we go into the basement to hang out. We're not there two minutes when Erin bounds down the stairs. Zoe's behind her. She waves at me.

"Hi. Uh, how was your trip?" I ask.

She tilts her head. "Actually . . . better than I expected."

Erin plops onto the sofa. Her hair is sticking out in all directions. "Emergency meeting. I knew going into this that ZCIC would be like nothing I'd ever experienced before. But I didn't know it would be quite this nerve-racking."

Zoe sits next to her.

"Erin," I say. "Romanov is just a lot of talk. You let him get to you too easily. He's like a basketball player who brags about his skills all the time and annoys everyone."

"I hate that," Brian says. "It's ruined the game, if you want my opinion."

Erin sighs. "It's not only him. I walked around the tables this afternoon. I've never felt so intimidated in my life. You should hear what everyone's doing. I mean, you get in a group like this, with all these people, and you realize . . . I mean, you feel like you're not . . ."

"Erin, no," Zoe says.

She shakes her head. "Good enough."

Brian smirks. "Welcome to my world. I feel like that basically all the time."

"That's not true, and you can't think like that," Zoe says. "Then you'll never try anything."

Erin ignores her and looks up at me with a pained face. "Ethan, my little study device and your desk on a stick . . ."

I roll my eyes. "Let me guess. Not big enough?"

"Nowhere near."

Zoe leans forward. "Wait, desk on a stick? That's so cute."

"Thanks," I say. "Natalia and I came up with a whole new concept. It'll have wheels and—"

"Doesn't matter," Erin interrupts. "I could make a great device and you could make a terrific desk, but they're not going to cut it, not compared to what everyone else is doing. I mean, melting polar ice, okay? That's *big*."

"Wow," Zoe says. "What are they doing? I'd love to see that project."

Erin shrugs. "I don't know."

"You're wrong," I tell Erin. "My idea is good. Useful and new. It could make school so much better for a lot of kids! I'm talking millions."

"So will my idea, but I'm telling you—"

"People of the basement." Brian's leaning against the air hockey table with his arms crossed. "Are you listening to yourselves?" He's grinning like he got a joke no one else did. "Hello? Duh. You two want the same thing here."

"What are you talking about?" Erin frowns. "Our projects are completely different."

"Uh, no," Brian says. "They're not." He slaps a hand on top of the air hockey table. "We've been using the same desks in school for as long as this table's been around."

"Way longer," Erin goes.

Brian waves an arm. "Whatever. You get my point. And kids use the same old assignment notebooks year after year, am I right?"

"Okay," I say.

"Both of you want to make school better for kids." Brian points to me. "Have a standing desk." He looks at Erin. "Keep track of your assignments."

Erin and I glance at each other.

Zoe leaps up. "Brian, you're a genius!"

"Yeah, yeah." He does a little swagger and brushes a hand across his shoulder. "I like to keep that side of me hidden. You know, not brag about my geniusness. Is that a word?"

Zoe bobs her head excitedly. "Little things add up to big things!"

"What exactly are you guys saying?" Erin asks.

Brian pushes the puck across the air hockey table. It slides into the goal slot. He holds up the two strikers. "Team up."

"Team up?" I repeat.

Zoe claps. "Yes! That's exactly what you should do!"

Erin stares at them. "This is probably completely against the rules, totally illegal, you guys helping us. But you know what? I don't care! I DON'T CARE."

Brian raises his eyebrows. "Whoa, Erin McB! Ready to go to ZCIC prison."

"What do you think?" Erin asks me.

"I don't need to team up! I want to do *my* idea. I like it. It's good! We've put a lot of work into it."

Erin stands and starts pacing. Her cheeks are flushed and her eyes are glistening. "You *can* do your idea, and you will. Don't you see?" She stops in front of me.

"No."

"We'll figure out a way to incorporate *both* of our projects together into something bigger!"

"Uh-uh. You'll take over," I say. "You'll change it."

"I won't."

"Right," I mutter. Brian and Zoe are on Erin's side, I can tell. They're all looking at me, waiting for me to get *on board*. What just happened? How did this spiral out of control so fast? And is Erin right? Will my invention not cut it? Do I even care about that, or do I only care about making something better than before?

"Well?" Erin asks.

"Dude," Brian says. "You gotta know when to fold 'em."

I care. About the first thing.

"I'm only agreeing to this if we keep my desk on a stick. Tell me we're keeping it. Promise, and *stick* to it this time. And you're gonna listen to me, not just do it your way."

"Yes, yes." Erin holds up her palm. "I promise. And you have to listen to me, too."

"Okay, then, I guess—"

Erin twirls around, Zoe shouts, "Yay!" and Brian goes, "You're welcome."

A smile spreads across my sister's face. "Ethan, remember the guest speaker on the second day? What he said it was about and what we should focus on?"

"Uh, no . . ."

"He said it wasn't about learning to code or winning or selling your invention, or anything like that. He said it was about the idea. Just the idea. Now you remember?"

"Yeah, now I do."

"This," she says, softly punching my shoulder. "This is the idea. *Our* idea."

"Hey," Brian interrupts. "*My* idea. I was the one who thought of you guys teaming up, like, two minutes ago, remember?"

Erin looks at him. "Yes. Thank you."

CHAPTER TWENTY-THREE

Again

M.R.

After dinner, I play chess. I am my own opponent.

Mom comes over, rests a hand on my shoulder. "Marlon. I have some news."

I know before she says it.

"We are moving again. Dad got the word today."

"Will I be able to finish the school year here?"

"I'm afraid not. They need him there as soon as possible." She sits next to me. "I know it must be hard on you, leaving your school and classmates again and again." She runs a finger across the wood table, tracing a lighter part of the grain. "Truth be told, it's getting hard on me, too."

We sit for a few minutes, both of us quiet. I make a last move. A knight. "Checkmate," I whisper, and Mom pats my back. "It will be okay," she says.

I nod.

"This is what we do," she says, then gets up, brushes her skirt. "What else can we do?" She goes into the kitchen.

I return the chess pieces to their starting positions, placing them neatly in their squares, then walk down the hall to my small, tidy room. I survey the contents. A bed, a dresser, a desk. Clothes and shoes in the closet. My Shakespeare volume.

When you move frequently, you learn not to carry many items with you. They only take up space in a truck. You learn what is truly necessary, and you learn to be ready at a moment's notice.

I hear running water in the bathroom, the creak of a floor, the sound of a car horn blaring outside. Sounds of a place I will not remember. I hear my father's laugh and my mother's optimistic voice. They are already discussing, planning, starting to prepare. That is what they do.

I wonder where we are going. I did not ask.

Does it matter?

In chess, the king is arguably the most important piece, yet also the weakest. A player must always protect the king. He is most vulnerable.

I find that interesting.

I wanted you to know.

CHAPTER TWENTY-FOUR

The Innovative Four

ETHAN

After Zoe and Brian leave, Erin and I shut off the lights and go upstairs. Mom and Dad are already in bed. We stand in the hall for a few minutes, a bright full moon visible through the window at the top of the hallway, our shadows long across the carpet.

"Brian," I say, shaking my head.

"I know. I can't believe it," Erin replies.

"The guy might annoy you to death, but you gotta admit, that was pretty brilliant. I mean, he saw something you and I never even thought of."

"It was shockingly perceptive. It never crossed my mind to team up."

"We were both too focused on doing our own thing."

She nods. "We were. So we'll talk to Connor and Natalia tomorrow morning about joining forces. Agree?"

"Agree."

"I hope they like the idea."

"I think they will."

We look at each other and smile. We know it. We can make something better together than apart. And this weird revelation occurs to me: Has it always been that way? Only we never realized it before because we were too busy arguing over little stuff? It took *Kowalski* to point that out?

"Well, see you in the a.m.," Erin says.

"Yep."

"We don't have a lot of time, you know. We're going to have to work quickly."

"We can do it."

She walks to her door, then turns back. "Yes. We can."

The next morning, once we're inside the atrium, we ask Connor and Natalia what they think about working as a team. It doesn't take much convincing. They get it immediately.

Natalia twirls a bracelet. "Makes absolute sense! We're both trying to improve the school experience."

Connor pushes up his glasses. "So you're saying we combine our projects somehow?"

Erin opens her briefcase. "Yes, and that's what we need to decide on. We have a desk on a stick and an assignment tracker device. How do we put them together?" She takes out a pile of papers. "I thought about this all night. I barely slept. More than two smaller things, we need a big thing. We basically need a brand-new take on the old, boring school-classroom environment. The way it's been for a hundred years. Desks and notebooks."

Natalia's eyes get wide, and she makes a small circle with her hands. "Wholeness!"

"Yes," Erin says. "I'm just going to run it by Jet, make sure it's okay this late in the game." She's back a few minutes later. "Full speed ahead. Time to brainstorm."

For the next hour we kick around ideas about standing desks and virtual study aids.

We talk about my desk-evator and chairs and stools and music stands. Connor shows us his Giga Pet, and we look at several homework apps. Erin summarizes her pages (and pages) of notes.

"It can't be expensive to make," she says. "Schools have to be able to afford this."

"Good point," Connor agrees.

Natalia swirls a finger around her tablet screen. "It doesn't have to be complicated. Something simple, but effective."

Erin frowns. "But it can't be *too* simple. It has to make an impact. A 'wow' kind of impression. The judges need to see its enormous potential right away."

"Just because something's simple doesn't mean it can't have an impact," Natalia protests. "In fact, it can have *more* of an impact."

"First and foremost," Connor interrupts, "it has to work."

"On board with that." I grin.

"Simple," Natalia repeats. "Like vanilla ice cream. Like a perfectly sweet orange."

Erin crosses her arms. "We're not talking about food. This absolutely has to stand out. Get it, *stand* out? If not, we're going nowhere."

"We don't have to go anywhere," Natalia replies. "Why

is it always about that? All we have to do is invent something we're proud of."

"Well, at the moment," Erin snaps, "we're not inventing anything. We're going in too many different directions."

Jet floats by our table. "How are we, Z people?"

"Good," Erin quickly answers. When he drifts away, she goes, "We need to focus. Get it together."

That's when it hits me. The bicycle. Simple, works, makes an impact. Yeah.

"Hey, everyone, we don't have to reinvent the wheel." I laugh. "Inside joke. Anyway, we've all done a lot of work. What if we made my desk on a stick like I planned, but we build your device into it? Like, there's a slot where it clips into the top? Maybe like a charging station?"

Connor's face lights up. "That's a really good idea. Why didn't I think of that?"

"I can completely visualize it!" Natalia says. "It'll be the desk of the future."

Erin nods slowly. "That's it. That's totally it."

Connor smiles and grabs his laptop. "Now, this is what I call fun."

Natalia reaches for our hands. "I feel so Zen, you guys! It's day four, and now we are four."

"The Four Innovators," Erin says. "Or the Innovative Four. I like that better."

"Doesn't matter what we're called," I say. "We need to make this. Now."

Connor powers up his laptop, and Erin powers up her mechanical pencil. Natalia holds her tablet on her lap. I stand in front of an invisible digital desk on a stick, imagining myself using it in Delman's classroom. I envision the height, the size, where the device would be located on the desktop.

Erin looks up at me. We nod at each other, and then the four of us huddle and get to work.

With only a small amount of additional group-project drama (because how could we not have that), by midafternoon we pretty much agree on the concept. Natalia's still dedicated to staying simple and Erin's still obsessed with a big impact, but I take on the role of team ref. Someone's gotta do it, right? Let's just say they now know the signs for foul, time-out, and jump ball.

With our input, Connor creates a virtual 3-D model.

It's a desk on a stand, with a tripod base and wheels. A movable top that slides up and down by twisting a knob. There's a stool that unfolds. Side slots for materials. And a touch-screen tablet that fits into each to track the assignments, test dates, and homework, plus link to teachers' web pages.

If this isn't the desk of the future, I don't know what is.

Erin claps a hand over her heart. "I love this. I love everything about it. It's innovative, creative, solves a problem in a fresh, new, updated way. And kids will love using it, don't you think?"

"Definitely," Connor says. "So here's the question. Do we build an actual model? We don't have a ton of time left. The presentations start tomorrow."

"We can do it," Erin says. "I'll start on the revised business plan right now."

"I'll work on the specific design," Natalia adds. "I'm thinking blue for harmony and yellow for imagination. Color is more powerful than people realize."

Connor stands, stretches his arms overhead. "I'll go see what I can dig up in the Zation room. Maybe we can at least make a rough prototype."

I smile. "I'm familiar with rough prototypes." Suddenly, as if on cue, I get a jolt of ESD. "I gotta take a break first, though." I tell Connor I'll find him in a few minutes.

I'm not sure if this is allowed, but I go out the front door. No one from the Z Team comes rushing after me. The fresh air feels great, and I decide to take a quick jog around the building. I turn to my right, then turn again when I reach the corner. The snow's deeper on this side, and my shoes get filled with snow in seconds. Okay, why do I do these things? I don't even think sometimes. I turn back and start jogging again; then, as I pass a window, I spot Z and Imani inside.

I stop and crouch under the window frame. Is that the room he went into in the off-limits hallway? I think it is! I slowly raise my head and peek inside.

I see a dry-erase board. Z and Imani are standing in front of it and pointing to things on the board. Their backs are to me. I squint. It's hard to make out, but I think I see names, and next to the names are words. *Hearing Aid. ER Robot. Drive-Thru Concept.* Next to the words are . . . I peer closer. Dollar signs? And some have, what are those, red check marks?

Then I see my name and Natalia's. And next to our names it says: *Standing School Desk*. There are two dollar signs.

Z puts a cap on a marker, then turns. In a panic I drop down to the ground and crawl through the snow until I'm at the front of the building. I run back inside and try to walk as calmly as possible to our table. When I reach it, I'm panting and sweating, and my shoes and socks and pant legs are soaked.

Erin eyes me up and down. "Oh my God! What happened to *you*?"

"I saw something," I whisper, my eyes darting around the atrium.

"What are you talking about?"

Natalia stares at me. "Your energy isn't good right now. I'm gathering a sense of unease."

"Something's weird," I hiss. "Something suspicious."

Erin raises an eyebrow. "Too many hours on Netflix, Ethan. Stop fooling around. We have so much to do."

I lower myself slowly until I'm squatting next to Erin's chair. "Listen to me, okay? Earlier in the week I overheard Z saying he couldn't talk to someone on the phone, and hadn't slept in weeks. Another time, he told someone 'there's no problem.' He sounded nervous. Then, just now—"

Connor comes to the table, holding a metal pole. "What's going on?"

I stand and motion for them to come closer. "I went outside to get some air. I was on the side of the building. I looked inside a room where Z and Imani had everyone's projects listed on a dry-erase board."

"So?" Erin says. "They're probably keeping track of each group's progress."

"There were dollar signs by each one."

Connor frowns. "Why would that be?"

"Exactly what I'm wondering," I say.

"Not getting any red flags here," Erin scoffs. "It could be anything. Like how much they think each project would sell for, or something like that."

"But remember, that speaker said it wasn't about selling your invention. So why the dollar signs? And there's another thing," I say. "Some of the projects had red check marks by them, and others didn't."

"What do you think that means?" Natalia asks.

I slip off my shoes, dump out some melted snow. "I don't know."

"Did you see yours?" Erin says, and I nod.

"Did it have a check mark?" she asks.

"Yeah, it did."

"Did you see mine?"

"I only looked for a few seconds. I had to run. Z turned toward the window."

She tips her head. "Was mine on there?"

"I didn't see it."

"Look, maybe they just . . . ," Natalia starts, but her voice trails off.

I stare in the direction of the off-limits hallway. "Something's up."

"I have the same feeling," Connor says. "But what?"

CHAPTER TWENTY-FIVE

Suspicious

ERIN

I don't know what Ethan thought he saw, but I'm sure it's all part of what they do here. Why *wouldn't* Z have a list of everyone's projects, with estimates of their value? They obviously need to keep track of what the groups are creating. And I'm sure mine was on there; Ethan just didn't see it. But anyway, it doesn't matter now. We've got something better.

Ethan and Connor start working on a physical model of our digital standing desk from materials they gathered in the Zation room, while Natalia and I address the business end. Ethan keeps shooting me looks, but I'm ignoring them and his wild imagination.

I put together an estimate of how much it would cost to make our desk, while Natalia works on how we'd promote and market the product to schools. I try a few different production variables, but the numbers keep coming out higher than I'd like.

"I wonder if we could get financial sponsors to foot the bill," I ask. "Companies would be all over this, don't you think?"

"Oh, I'm sure," Natalia agrees. "But no advertising or anything like that, right?"

"We're not even at that point."

"I'm just saying. We should keep that in mind."

"Most companies would want some sort of credit." Natalia needs to get out of her Zen area and into the future. I'm just saying.

I sit back and study what Ethan and Connor have made so far. There's a thin rectangular metal piece about the size of a three-ring binder that's secured to a pole. The piece slides up and down. Not so well, but it moves. The base seems pretty steady—it looks like it's from a microphone stand—and there are small, open boxes fastened to each side of the top (for supplies, I assume). They've also attached a canvas seat to the middle of the pole. Sort of like a folding stool you'd go camping with. Not that I've ever used one, but I've seen pictures.

Ethan sees me and puts up a hand. "It's rough. We know that. Don't say anything."

"At least there isn't any . . ."

He grins. "Duct tape."

"What?" Connor says. "Why would we use—"

"Inside joke," I answer, then turn to Natalia. "We need a better name for this."

She nods, then mouths, "Desk on a stick?"

At last she and I are on the same page with something. I roll my eyes. "I know. Let's not go there. We need a name to reflect the"—I smile at her—"wholeness. Should we keep 'desk of the future' or think of something catchier? Desktopia? Techno-desk?"

She fingers a braid. "Hmm. Or should we be clear and straightforward? Just DSD, for Digital Standing Desk?"

I laugh. "That's actually funny, because my dad calls Ethan's fidgeting ESD. Ethan Squiggle Disease."

Ethan leans toward us. "You talking about me?"

"What do you think of DSD?" I ask.

"Would people know what that is, though?"

Connor's securing a bolt with a screwdriver. "I wouldn't."

"Yeah," I say. "Me either."

Connor stops and holds the screwdriver. "What we're really doing here is making something to help students succeed. So what about . . . Desk for Success? A riff on 'dress for success,' get it?"

My mouth drops open. "Desk for Success! Connor, that's . . . Oh my God, that's perfect." First Brian, now Connor. What is happening in my world?

He bows. "Why, thank you."

I'm about to suggest an idea for a logo, but I look up, and Z is standing by our table. *Z*, inches from me! Imani is next to him, holding a tablet.

"Greetings," he says, towering above us like a skyscraper.

I'm not able to speak. Or move. Or, perhaps, breathe.

He waves a hand. "What have we here, Z people?"

Connor seems to be the only one who is able to function at the moment. "We're creating a new, state-of-the-art digital desk for school." He gestures to the model, perched unsteadily on the floor next to our table. "You can stand or sit. The top will have a space for a screen with assignments, links to teacher web pages, test dates.

It can be a personal whiteboard too. You'll have your own log-in. And you can't lose it, like your phone or an assignment notebook. It'll be right there in every class with you, part of the desk."

"Interesting," Z says. "Imani, weren't these two separate projects? The desk and the study aid?"

"Yes," she says, consulting her tablet.

"You've altered your concept, then?" Z asks.

Ethan narrows his eyes.

"Yeah. Jet said it was perfectly okay to combine our projects," Connor explains.

Natalia shows him her tablet, where she's drawn a model like Connor's, but it's in shades of blue and yellow. "Desk for Success," she says, beaming.

"Expensive to produce?" Z asks. "What's the profit margin?"

I clear my throat. "Um, we're still working that out, but we think companies or foundations might be interested in helping with the cost. Everyone wants kids to do well in school and keep up with the latest technology."

Z peers down at me, and I almost melt under his piercing sunglasses gaze.

"Please make a note of this, Imani," Z says, then looks back at us. "Thank you. Continue."

After he walks away, Ethan goes, "See!"

"See what?" I blink, trying to regain consciousness. "He just wanted to know what we were doing!"

"Didn't it seem a little suspicious, the way he asked if we changed our concept? How he had Imani check? Asked about profits? Why would he care about profits!"

"I don't know what you're getting at. Why is that suspicious?"

Ethan drums his fingers on the table and looks toward Z, standing at another table talking to some kids. "The guy's awfully concerned about money, if you ask me. That's not what this is supposed to be about."

Connor scratches the back of his neck. "He does have a creepy vibe up close. Why doesn't he take off the sunglasses? Ever?"

Natalia puts her palms together toward her heart. "I did feel something off-center with his energy. And I'm pretty spot-on about these things. I can tell my brother's mood just by looking at him."

"Z is very well respected and successful," I remind

them. "Everyone knows that. Whatever you're imagining about him, you're completely wrong. There's nothing suspicious going on, except him wanting to help kids and grow the future."

"I can't put my finger on it," Ethan says.

"Well, put it out of your mind. And your finger. We need to concentrate. Tomorrow is the big day. Our presentation. We need to be completely ready. Mentally, physically, emotionally. No distractions. C'mon, back to work."

ETHAN

That night I run over to Brian's. It's freezing, but I don't even bother with a jacket. No one else is listening to me, except Connor, a little. I gotta get Kowalski's take on this.

We can't go into his room since his grandma's living in there now. He motions toward his brother's room. "John went to a movie. Don't touch anything. He'll know." Brian shuts the door. "What's the emergency? Did Erin murder someone at the camp?"

"Ha. Very funny. No, this is serious."

"Yeah? Lay it on me."

I pace around the room. "So, Zak Canzeri, he's all successful and everyone acts like he's king of the tech universe, but I think the guy isn't what he seems."

"How come?"

I tell Brian what I overheard and what I saw.

"I'm not sure I'm getting any criminal activity from that," he says.

I wave my arms, accidentally knocking a picture frame out of place. Brian straightens it. "Erin thinks I'm crazy. Like I'm imagining stuff."

"She always thinks you're crazy. She thinks everyone's crazy."

"And the truth is, Z's creepy. He wears dark sunglasses all the time and appeared in a puff of smoke, like a magician. I can't explain it, and I guess I don't have much to go on. Just, you know how you get a feeling about something and you can't shake it?"

"Uh-huh."

"I have that feeling."

"What's your gut saying?"

"I don't know, but those dollar signs are bugging me. Why would he put those next to the projects?"

He shrugs. "My dad says money runs the world. They probably pick the winner based on who's gonna make the most money."

"That doesn't make sense, though. All they talk about is TADA and the *idea*, right, not making money."

"Yeah, and you believe that?" Brian says. "I wouldn't be surprised if Z sells kids' ideas or something."

I stare at Brian. "What did you just say?"

"I said I wouldn't be surprised if Z—"

"I heard you. He couldn't do that. Could he do that?"

"How would I know? I was just—"

My phone buzzes and I pull it from my pocket. It's a text from Zoe: Can we talk? I show the phone to Brian.

"Man, you got some heavy stuff goin' on," he says, laughing. "I'm really glad I didn't go to that camp. And I'm kinda glad I don't have a girlfriend. Way too complicated."

I shove the phone back into my pocket. I can't deal with it right now.

Brian goes over to the window, unlocks it, and cranks it open. A cold breeze hits the room. "I asked Gram what's with the spitting. She has a pierogi for a brain, but you know what she answered? She said spitting clears out the cobwebs. I ask you, does that not make sense?"

"It makes sense, in a strange way."

Brian pops out the screen. "When you don't know what else to do . . ."

I grin. "Spit in the wind?"

He motions to me and I walk over. "On three," he says.

We both gather the saliva in our mouths. Brian holds up one, two, then three fingers. We hurl two spits down at the snow, watch them land. Definitely respectable, actually quite massive spits.

"Feel better?" he asks.

"Weirdly, I kinda do."

He closes the window. "For the second time this week, you're welcome."

CHAPTER TWENTY-SIX

The Woodpecker

ZOE

I'm in my room, writing Dad a letter. I want to write, not text or e-mail. There are some things I need to say, and they need to be in ink, on paper. (Recycled paper.) And I don't want to hear his answers right away. If they come.

Mom and Hannah are baking cookies. I can hear them in the kitchen. Mom: "If you eat too much of the dough, you're going to get a stomachache!" Hannah: "I don't care!" Mom laughs; then Hannah does too.

They call me, and I say I'll be there in a minute.

> Dear Dad,
> I hope you're happy with Dara. I would like to meet her one day. Maybe you can come and visit after the baby is born.

I was mad at you for a long time. I
was mad you left, and mad you left us.
But we're doing fine now. I thought you
might want to know.
Also, I wondered if you still love me. I
don't know if you do, but I want to tell
you that I still love you.
Zoe

I put the letter into an envelope and seal it. Then I go downstairs and look out the front window. It's clear, and the sky is that deep navy color just before it turns black. There's an icicle hanging from the mailbox. I hope the woodpecker is warm and cozy inside.

I go outside and tiptoe toward the mailbox, then put my ear close and listen.

Nothing. It's too quiet.

I slowly open the little door and peek inside. It's empty. Just one black feather. I pick it up and feel the softness between my fingers.

Has the woodpecker left for good? I search the trees around our house, hoping to see him perched against a trunk or hear his rhythmic tapping. But I think he's gone.

Why did he live in our mailbox for those few short weeks? Why was he here?

I look up at the sky and take in the stars at last. I've missed them. I remember something Dad told me on our last nature hike. "The universe holds mysteries that the human brain can't begin to comprehend."

I didn't know it would be our last. Maybe he did.

That was also when he said I would be a great scientist one day. That I would discover a cure, or figure out a solution to slow climate change. That I would—and he laughed here, because it's become such a cliché—make a difference in the world.

"You really think so?" I asked.

"Absolutely," he answered. "No doubt."

I toss the feather into the air and watch it drift down to the snowy ground. Tiny and black against the vast whiteness.

I turn my face up to the stars and think about the mysteries of life. And the meaning of Zoe.

I think it's okay to love someone without knowing if

they love you back. Or if they used to love you but maybe forgot. If love is there, then it's there for good.

A gust of wind picks up the feather, and it sails away. I watch until I can't see it anymore. Then I hurry inside. Cookies are waiting.

CHAPTER TWENTY-SEVEN

Flying

ETHAN

When Erin comes into the kitchen on the last morning of ZCIC, she's wearing gray pants and a dark blue suit-ish jacket, and Mom's shoes. Her hair is completely straight, sort of pasted to her scalp, and she's got a mean-looking bright red mark on her forehead.

She jerks opens the fridge. "Don't say anything!"

I don't dare.

She whirls around. "If you must know, I flat-ironed my hair this morning and accidentally burned my forehead." She grabs an apple, shuts the fridge, then starts arranging things in her briefcase.

Mom and Dad both drive us, and apparently, they feel it's a good choice not to mention Erin's forehead either.

"Go out there today and hit a home run," Dad says as we arrive at Gotham City.

Mom turns around. "But of course I don't have to tell you, it's not about whether you win or lose. It's about the journey, right? We're proud of you no matter what." She winks at us. "Text me, though, anyway, okay? I admit I'm dying to know who wins."

"Sure," I answer. Erin's already out of the car.

When we get inside, Jet announces that we have about twenty minutes for our final touches before everyone starts presenting to the panel of investors, industry experts, and of course Z himself.

Natalia peers at Erin. "Would you like me to put a dab of essential oil on that red mark? I think lavender would help calm the skin."

Erin's hand flies to her forehead. "No, thank you. It'll be fine."

Connor and I take a last look at the Desk for Success. We couldn't really put a screen on the top, but we have Natalia's tablet on it to demonstrate the concept. We got the top piece to slide up and down better (Connor figured that out, don't ask me how) and made the whole thing steadier by adding another leg to the pop-out stool. I think it looks awesome.

Erin flips through her notes and quietly rehearses our presentation, talking and gesturing to herself. I don't think any of us had to vote on who's going to speak on behalf of the Innovative Four.

"It's time, Z people," Jet announces. "Let the final lap begin."

We're ushered into what was the Zation room, but now there are three men and three women sitting at a long table in the front, a microphone on a stand, and chairs set up in rows facing the table. The judges, I guess they are, have name cards in front of them.

Erin's *ooh*ing and *aah*ing. "These people are super important," she whispers.

Of course they are. Except, how come I've never heard of them?

There's an empty seat in the middle with a gold *Z* on the back of the chair. "I wonder who that's for," I mutter, and Erin shushes me.

Jet makes this speech about how amazing the week was, how we're all amazing kids, and we have amazing futures ahead of us. He says "amazing" about twenty more times. Imani, Asher, and Maddox are standing next to him, bobbing their heads in unison. I realize they're all the same exact height. Another weird thing.

Then Z makes his entrance. He glides into the room, goes to the Z chair, and stands behind it. Everyone applauds until he finally sits. Black shirt, sunglasses. At least the guy keeps it consistent.

The first group is called to present. It's the kids who are creating the improved hearing aid. They each take a turn speaking, going over the device and explaining how it's better than what's currently in use. They even do a demonstration of how it feels when you lose your hearing.

The judges ask them some questions and make notes. Z says nothing.

The kid with the I AM THE FUTURE cap is up second. He hasn't taken off that cap once the entire week. His future is apparently in drive-thrus. No kidding. He's created a completely computerized process for fast-food places. He even sings a couple of jingles and asks the judges to guess which restaurants they belong to. They look very entertained by that, but I spot Erin rolling her eyes.

More presentations—everything from climate-change

solutions to "huts for the homeless" to a robot that can take people's vital signs in an emergency room—then it's time for a lunch break. Everyone goes into the atrium. I'm starving, but Erin says she's not hungry. She presses a hand against her stomach. "I feel sick."

I grab a piece of bread from the buffet and offer it to her. "Mom would tell you to eat something. You'll feel better."

"No. I can't." She stumbles toward the door.

Connor takes off his glasses, rubs the side of his nose. "Is she gonna bail on us?"

"Maybe some ylang-ylang oil," Natalia suggests.

"No." I shove the bread into my mouth. "I'll handle this."

Erin's standing outside the front door without her coat on, and she doesn't look so good. Her face has a green-ish tinge, except for the red mark, and she looks like she might puke right onto the sidewalk.

"I'm not okay," she says.

"How can you not be okay? You've, like, trained for this your entire life. Remember how excited you were when you got the invite? We have a big project, Erin. I know we do! It's good! Don't start doubting."

She looks at me. Her forehead is all wrinkly. "Ethan . . . listen to me. I know how to study. Do assignments. Excel on tests. But this . . . this is the real world. These kids here—what I've realized this week—I'm not like that. Planning, researching, and organizing is one thing. Being an innovator is another. They have something I don't have. Maybe it's TADA, I don't know."

"Erin, you'll be fine. You always are. C'mon, let's go back in."

She doesn't reply. Or move.

"Hey, I know you're gonna get up there and wow the judges and make everything sound great. You were awesome when you said all that stuff to Mr. Delman after the stand-in!"

She blows out a breath.

"Good. Breathing is good. And we need to do something else right now. Just go with me here, okay?"

"What?"

"We're gonna spit."

"I'm not doing that. You know I don't spit."

I elbow her. "Rin, trust me."

"Spitting is gross. It's a disgusting habit."

"Trust me," I repeat, then smile. "I did it last night at Brian's. His gram is the real genius. I swear. She said it clears the cobwebs." I gather the saliva in my mouth and spit on the grass.

"Oh, fine!" She makes this loud gurgling sound and shoots out a giant wad of spit. It lands on a snow-covered bush.

I clap. "How do you feel?"

She pats her mouth with the end of her sleeve, then burps. "Better, for some unexplainable reason."

"Told ya. Now let's go." I take her arm and practically drag her through the door. I grab some food from the buffet and wolf it down, but Erin says she still can't eat. Then lunch is over and we're up.

Our model is at the front of the room, and Natalia's blue-and-yellow virtual design is projected onto a screen. We all stand in front of the judges, and Erin walks unsteadily to the microphone. "Hello," she says. The microphone reverberates because she's too close. "Sorry." She steps back. "Um, we are the Innovative Four, and our project is . . ." She looks over at me and I give her a thumbs-up.

"Our project is the Desk for Success. Research shows that students . . ."

One of the judges looks down at her phone.

Erin swallows. "Sitting in school is a real problem, and so is keeping track of your assignments and test dates." Another judge crosses his arms. Erin shifts her feet, clears her throat. The room is silent.

My sister saved me in LA when she got everyone to stand up and protest. Now it's my turn to save her. I walk to the microphone. Erin starts to step aside, but I grab her arm. "Together," I say.

"Together," she whispers.

"Desk for Success," I announce. "Unique, inventive, groundbreaking. Please turn your attention to our virtual model and physical prototype, and I will walk you through it."

And then I just go. Give the smoothest speech of my life. You do things like that when you have to.

Erin doesn't look green and wrinkly anymore. She leans in and adds a few details at just the right moments. We're like, well, Orville and Wilbur.

Mom and Dad questioned me, and Erin said I

wouldn't survive, but I did. My invitation wasn't a mistake, and I'm not the slacker example.

I belonged here and I did this.

With, okay, yeah, a little help from my sister and Connor and Natalia.

And at the end of my talk, are you ready for this? Z lowers those freakin' sunglasses, tilts his head, and looks directly at me for the briefest second. He slides them back up, but I saw his eyes. They're light brown, with this sort of yellowish rim. And you know what they made me think of? This might creep you out, but a coyote's eyes. I once saw one by our house, and I swear, it had eyes just like Z's.

CHAPTER TWENTY-EIGHT

And the Winner Is . . .

ETHAN

The judges ask a few questions. Connor answers one; I answer another. We sit down, and Romanov is called next.

Connor low-fives me. "Couldn't have done better myself."

"Namaste," Natalia whispers, applauding softly.

Erin touches my arm and nods.

I grin, shrug. "Yeah, yeah."

"You guys are actually pretty tight," Connor says. "Even if you don't think so."

Erin and I give each other a quick smile. Sometimes, I guess, we are. When we need to be. When it counts. Like now.

Romanov starts his presentation. He talks sort of stiffly, but it doesn't matter. Once he explains his project, the judges aren't fiddling around or acting distracted. They're paying 100 percent attention.

He's created a virtual model of a device he says will be possible in the very near future. It'll be a tiny unit you wear on your forehead, resembling a small microphone that actors use onstage, and it will augment your thinking. You won't have to tell it what to do or what you need; it will *know*.

"It is called," Romanov says, "FRIEND. Simply put, FRIEND will help you navigate the world better than you can on your own. This isn't artificial intelligence; it is your intelligence, magnified. It will harness the power of your brain. Increase its capacity and abilities. And it may be able to detect and stop dementia."

Erin's staring at him, her mouth open slightly.

I'm lost in two seconds, as Romanov talks about neurons and sensory input and object recognition and electrical impulses. When he finishes, the judges seem too stunned to ask questions, but Z actually stands. "You came up with this yourself?" he asks.

"Yes," Romanov says.

"You didn't copy this idea from something you read online, perhaps? There are things like this being researched, I believe."

Romanov shakes his head.

Z nods once. "Thank you."

The rest of the kids present; then we have a short break while the judges decide on the winners.

Connor, Natalia, Erin, and I hang out in a corner of the atrium. "That's it," Erin says. "What do they have to decide? Marlon's the winner."

"FRIEND is pretty amazing," Connor says. "If it's possible. I think it'll be a while before something like that is. There were some other strong projects. My money's on that ER robot."

"Money," I say, smirking a little.

Natalia hands Connor and Erin energy bands, and Erin accepts hers this time. "However this ends up," Natalia says, "it was a truly enriching experience to be the Innovative Four."

"Yeah," Connor agrees, then asks where Erin and I live. Erin tells him; then he says he's not that far from us. "We'll have to make plans sometime," Connor says.

Natalia smiles. "New Year's Eve is tomorrow! Is anyone doing anything?"

"I'm in," I say. "We have a great basement."

"Maybe," Erin says, rubbing her stomach. "Let's get through this first."

A few minutes later Jet calls us to come back in for the "Zannouncement."

"Okay," I say, "whatever goes down, I think we did our best." I sound like Dad. Or worse, Mom.

We file in, take our seats. Z has the microphone. He thanks us for our hard work and outstanding presentations, then announces third place—the hearing-aid group—and everyone applauds. Second place is the emergency-room robot. Two girls go up to accept their trophy.

"And the winner," Z says, "is Marlon Romanov, for FRIEND."

"He won," Erin says, over the applause. "He said he would win and he did."

Romanov goes up to shake the judges' hands and pose for photos. Even now he's not smiling. It quickly becomes a mob scene, as kids crowd around. Erin stands. "He won," she repeats. Then she moves toward the front of the room. I'm watching her. She's going toward . . . Romanov.

Oh no. What's she gonna do now? Demand a recount? Punch the guy? I can't look, but I do. And my sister, with her pasted-on straight hair, red mark on her forehead, and Mom's unsteady high-heel shoes, pushes through the crowd, goes right up to him, and says something. It doesn't look like she's yelling. No punches are thrown. Then Marlon says something to her.

She comes back a minute later.

"What'd you just do?" I ask.

"I congratulated him."

"You did?"

"Yes. I—I realized something when they announced his name and not mine."

"What?"

She blinks back tears. "It didn't hurt as bad as I thought it would. I was invited to ZCIC, wasn't I? It's not about Marlon, or anyone else at the camp."

Connor nods. "Not that I'm saying I told you so, but I am."

I raise my hand. "Clueless again."

"Just something I pointed out to Erin. Even though I think she knew it."

Erin gulps, looks at Natalia. "I might've had a Zen moment."

Natalia hugs Connor. "Ethan told me you weren't supposed to be here. But you were! And this is why. To help Erin work through this issue she's had with Marlon."

Erin wipes her eyes and then smiles. "Truthfully, you guys, I think it was the spitting."

"Ha!" I say. "I knew it! So, what did Marlon answer?"

"He just said . . . thank you."

Z's talking into the microphone. "Attention. If I could have a word with the Innovative Four in the conference room?"

We all look at each other.

"Did we do something wrong?" Erin says.

"What's going on?" Connor adds.

I watch Z leave. "Let's go see."

Imani ushers us into a room around the corner from the atrium, then closes the door. Z's standing at one end. It's just the four of us, and him.

"Well done," Z says. "Quite impressive. The Innovative

Four. I like that. Sit. Make yourselves comfortable." We pull out chairs and he continues. "Unfortunately, your Desk for Success didn't win. But we do something special here at ZCIC. A select offer to those we feel have a superb idea."

Erin creases her brows and tilts her head, just like Mom does when she's confused about something.

"I'd like to offer you what we call a development fee. A Z fee."

I jab Erin as Connor repeats, "A Z fee?"

Z puts his fingertips together and makes a sort of dome with his hands. "I'd like to look into developing your idea. I'll reward you with an amount you'll find quite generous, I'm sure. I believe it has potential. However, you certainly wouldn't have the resources to put this into production, market it to schools, publicize it, et cetera."

I almost fall out of my chair. Brian was onto something! I stare at Z. He's not a maker; he's a *faker*! If anyone can spot a faker, it's me, the king of duct tape. And right in front of me is one *big*, smooth-talking, phony, sunglasses-wearing faker.

Connor asks, "How much are we talking about?"

But before Z answers, Erin bolts up. "Just a second! This is sort of unethical, don't you think?"

"Not at all," Z says calmly. "You came up with the idea; I am buying it from you. Happens all the time. It's the way the world works."

Erin's face goes pale. "But it's our idea. Our project. Would you give us credit?"

Z shrugs. I'll take that as a no.

Erin looks like she's half in shock, half disgusted.

"Actually, I—my family—could use the money," Connor says.

"Precisely," Z replies, smiling with his mouth closed.

"Have you done this before?" Erin asks in a low voice. "Developed a kid's project from your camp?"

"As I said, it's how the world works, my dear. Success is success, however it happens. In collaboration with others, or on your own."

Erin drops back into her chair. "My brother was right. I didn't believe him. I didn't *want* to believe him."

Z raises an eyebrow above his sunglasses.

Erin shakes her head. "TADA. The future generation. Do you even care about all that?" She gets up. "If this is good enough for your development fee, then we can find an investor who'll actually partner with us. Not pay us off. It's *our* idea." She jerks open the door and marches out of the room.

"The money woulda been nice," Connor says, "but we'd all have to agree. I can live without it." He goes out too. Natalia looks at Z, then at me. "Didn't I say there's always a catch with magicians?" She leaves, and then it's just me and him.

"Your sister will learn," Z says.

I move to the door. "I think she already has."

"Well then, good luck to you. No hard feelings, my friend."

I could say lots of things. Like that he's not my friend, or that I'm gonna tell everyone what he tried to do. Is it unethical, or how the world works? I'm not sure.

I stop, my hand on the doorknob, and turn back. "This whole time, I kept wondering what was up with the sunglasses. It's a little thing, but it really bothered me. I think I get it now. And, Mr. Canzeri? They're not working. People will see you. I did."

CHAPTER TWENTY-NINE

A Donut

M.R.

My name is announced. I rise to my feet, walk to the front of the room, and shake Z's hand. He gives me a gold Z-shaped trophy. We take pictures. Then the others—Jet, Imani, Asher, Maddox—also shake my hand and pat my shoulder and congratulate me. Excellent, they say. Well done. Impressive.

Erin Marcus approaches, and my stomach flutters, but she, too, offers me congratulations. I say thank you.

I have won.

I have taken first place. As I strived for. As I planned. As I knew I should.

One of the investors pumps my hand vigorously and says she would like to talk more about FRIEND. "It's a whole new horizon," she says. "Isn't it?"

I open my mouth to answer, but the sounds of the room grow louder in my ears. Not just words, but colors, too many dizzying, blurred colors. My palms become sweaty. My heart rate accelerates.

"A new horizon," I repeat.

My voice doesn't sound right. It echoes; it is far away. She is waiting for me to continue. At first patiently. Then, when I don't say anything, her expression changes. She blinks, tilts her head, looks at me questioningly.

I run from the room, rush through the atrium, and push open the front door to the building. Then I am outside in the cold. The smell of pine. A squirrel. Two birds. The blue sky.

My breath releases in small bursts. Tiny clouds that quickly dissipate.

The door opens behind me. Maddox is suddenly at my side. "Hey," she says.

I look into the sky. I observe the squirrel, leaping across the snow with seemingly no purpose. "It does not feel as I imagined."

She stuffs her hands into the pockets of her coat. "Winning, you mean?"

I nod. "Winning."

She laughs. A short, sharp sound. "It never does."

The squirrel circles a tree, then dashes up the trunk.

"You know I won the very first Z camp?" Maddox says.

"No, I did not."

"Yep. I was just like you. In your shoes, so to speak."

"And?"

She shrugs. "I sold my idea, made a few bucks."

"How did it do?"

"You mean in the real world? The investor never developed it." She takes out a hand, jerks her thumb toward the building. "But I got a job here right out of college, so that was good."

"Your idea was not developed?"

"Correct."

"I do not understand."

"Listen, Marlon, it's really great that you won. Huge congrats. You should feel proud. But at the end of the day, what is it, really? You're still just one person on this very large, complex planet."

We stand, silent for a few moments. My breath. Hers. Tiny clouds.

"Being gifted can be a crummy gift sometimes, can't it?"

"Yes," I say.

"I used to think that all the time too. Then I decided to forget about it." She pulls open the door. "You like donuts?"

"Donuts? I don't eat them. They have no nutritional value."

She smiles. "Why does that matter? What would you like? Chocolate? Powdered sugar? I can nab one from Z's private stash."

"But we have eaten only healthy food this week. Jet said it was 'food for the brain.'"

"Uh-huh, right. Z is a fanatical donut maniac. He can't live without his sugar high. But you didn't hear that from me." She motions. "Come on."

I hesitate.

"I'm offering you a free donut here. I don't know anyone who'd pass that up." She holds the door, and we go inside. It is calmer. The melee has dispersed. I do not see Mr. Canzeri anywhere.

"Don't go bolting outside again. I'll be right back,"

Maddox says. A few minutes later she returns with a gleaming chocolate donut on a napkin and hands it to me. "Better than the trophy, right?" She leans close. "You're a brilliant guy. But take it from me: just go be a person on this planet." She turns, and joins the rest of the Z Team at the far end of the atrium.

I take a bite. It is delicious. Four more bites and it's gone.

I retrieve my laptop, my headphones, the trophy, my materials. Pack everything into my bag, then exit the building. Mom is out front. I get into the car and hold up the trophy. She is so proud, she says. And then we pull away, begin the drive home. Along with every other car on the road. Everyone going somewhere.

Mom looks at me. "What's on the side of your mouth?"

I bring my fingers to my mouth, come away with a smear of sweet, sticky brown. I lick the icing from my fingers.

Later, I discover that donuts were invented in 1847, although some dispute that historical reference. And this thought occurs to me: What if they had been around in Shakespeare's day? How his plays might have been different had he been able to enjoy a chocolate donut once in a while.

I put the trophy on my desk next to the Shakespeare volume. As you know, I have read it through twice.

Perhaps that is enough.

Perhaps, when I arrive at my next school, I will leave it at home.

CHAPTER THIRTY

New Year's Eve

ERIN

Yes, I got up there and completely froze. And yes, I'm devastated. Not about that so much as about what Z did.

When we got home after the last day of camp, I searched "Zak Canzeri" online. Not the ZCIC website—*him*. Turns out, he hasn't had a success in a couple of years. One article even had this title: "Has Z's Star Burned Out?" Apparently, the investors with his new venture think he's "all talk and no action."

So, currently, I am searching for a new role model. I am actually considering—don't laugh—my brother.

Ethan and I are having a New Year's Eve party. Dad went down to the basement and got rid of the spiders. Mom and I strung party lights from the wood beams on the ceiling. We put a tablecloth over the air hockey table, so now it has a purpose at last—a place to put food and beverages. It looks quite festive, even though it's still a basement underneath all that. But things are not always what they seem, right?

We're not having a ton of people. Zoe, Brian. Natalia. And Connor.

I haven't really had time to process everything that happened during the camp, since it just ended yesterday, but I'll say that nothing was what I expected. I thought I would feel angry, jealous, and resentful that Marlon took first. But surprisingly, I don't.

I think it's because Marlon's invention was good. Brilliant, even. And I knew it. Everyone knew it.

Don't get me wrong. I think the Desk for Success has amazing potential. Dad says he has a manufacturing client who might want to set up a meeting with us to discuss the idea. I told Dad I was thrilled to hear that, then mentioned to Mom that I need to get a pair of professional heels that fit my feet, pronto. And, hopefully, by the time we meet, my forehead burn will be healed.

The doorbell rings, and when I open it, Connor's standing there. He comes in, hands me a plate covered in plastic wrap.

"What's this?" I ask.

"This would be Swedish meatballs."

"Oh. Did your mom make them?"

"Nope."

"Your dad?"

"Guess again."

"You?"

He grins, takes off his jacket. "It's an old family recipe that I made up this morning."

"You're . . . Swedish?"

He laughs. "I was kidding."

I carry the plate to the basement and he follows me. I make a space for it on the air hockey table. A few minutes later Natalia arrives, then Zoe. I introduce them. They bond instantly.

Brian careens down the stairs and more or less crashes into the room. He's wearing a glittery HAPPY NEW YEAR hat. He takes it off, waves it in the air, then pulls a noisemaker from his pocket and blows it. "I'm here! Start the party!"

Ethan puts on some music. He made a playlist. I don't recognize the first song, but he says it's by ZZ Top, an old band that Dad told him about. "It's kinda fitting, don't you think? The Z tie-in?"

We hang out for a while, not doing all that much; then, when I'm by the air hockey table, checking if anything needs to be refilled, Connor's suddenly next to me.

"Hi," he says.

"Hi."

"So, hey." He pushes up his glasses. "You wanna do something sometime? Maybe, like, see a movie?"

I pause. Is he asking me out? I study his face, try to determine what's going on. I can't tell. Why can't I tell?

"Possibly," I reply.

He grins, claps a hand to his chest. "That's your answer? Possibly? What's the deal breaker?"

"I'll have to think about that."

"You mean Person in Charge doesn't have a plan when a guy asks her out?"

So he is asking me out. Um, okay, wow.

"I just thought about it," I say. "What kind of movies do you like?"

"So that's a yes?"

I nod.

"Cool. I like old movies, from the fifties, sixties, seventies."

"I don't think I've ever seen a movie that old."

"Well, that has to change," he says.

Maybe so.

ZOE

It's weird and awkward and stiff between me and Ethan, and I don't like it. I feel like he's avoiding me. He never answered my text about talking. I'm trying not to look at him when he says something funny and everyone else laughs. We keep sort of stepping around each other.

Finally there's a moment when he's alone. Not goofing around with one of the guys, and not talking to someone. It's either now or this weirdness goes on the whole night. And it's New Year's! I can't start a year like this.

I motion for him to follow me to a corner of the basement. "I just want to say I'm sorry if I was all over you these past few weeks. I have a lot going on, with my mom and my dad and everything. I was trying to . . . I thought if I . . . Forget it. Whatever. Not important. It's okay if you don't like me. But we can be friends, right? I'd be sad if we weren't friends."

Ethan smiles. "You're friend-zoning me?"

I smile back at him. "I guess I am."

He gently knocks his fist on my shoulder. "I can live with that."

I want so badly to reach out and hug him, but I don't. We stand there for a few seconds. "So, funniest thing," I say finally. "There was a woodpecker living in our mailbox, but now he moved out."

"Really?"

"Did you know that woodpeckers tap between eight and twelve thousand times a day?"

"No. Doesn't that hurt their heads?"

"Uh-uh, they're uniquely built for that. Don't you love that about the perfection of nature?"

He laughs. "Definitely. You know what else is the perfection of nature?"

"What?"

"Those meatballs Connor made. I've had four."

"I'll have to try one."

"What! You haven't? Get over here."

Ethan grabs my arm and pulls me toward the air hockey buffet table, then stabs a meatball with a toothpick and hands it to me. I put it into my mouth, chew, swallow. "Good," I say.

"Good? How about awesomely excellent."

I look around their basement. The lights, the warmth, all of us here together on the brink of a brand-new year. "Okay," I say. "Awesomely excellent."

BRIAN

You aren't gonna believe this in a million freakin' years. I was all ready to forget about ever having a girlfriend. Then Natalia starts talking to me. And I'm not gonna get too worked up about it (okay, I am—I mean, how can I not?), but I think she LIKES me.

You want proof?

1) She taught me a yoga pose. The tree. You stand straight and tall, then bend one leg and clamp it to the other leg, by your thigh. Then you raise up your arms. She said I was really good at it, that I have great focus and balance.

2) She laughed at one of my lamest jokes. And believe me, it was *lame*.

3) She's doing that eyelash-fluttering thing that Zoe does when she looks at Ethan. And she's looking at ME.

Me!

Maybe, huh? Whaddya think?

Anyway, gotta go. She's gonna teach me a yoga pose called the warrior.

Hey, I can be a warrior. And into yoga. Whatever it takes.

ETHAN

I didn't flop. I didn't embarrass myself at the camp. And no one laughed at me . . . that I'm aware of. No, no one did. I'm sure of it.

We didn't win, but we made something really awesome. And let me say it again, loud and clear: NO DUCT TAPE!

And now, all this.

All this because I got a bad case of ESD and stood up in class one day.

Weird, huh?

It's a good thing Erin didn't finish our report for Mrs. D, because now we have to change it. What, you didn't think I was gonna forget about the Desk for Success, did you?

I have no idea if anything's gonna happen with our project, but you know something? Brian's gram is way smarter than anyone.

'Cause when you spit into the wind, I think it creates some sort of cosmic shift in the universe. Or you just get rid of excess saliva and clear away cobwebs that you didn't even know were clouding your brain. Either way, if you're ever in need, give it a try. It won't be what you expect.

Trust me.

ACKNOWLEDGMENTS

I DECIDED I WANTED TO BE A WRITER WHEN I WAS in fifth grade. That's about the time all big decisions are made, right? I wrote my first book that year—*The Chair That Knew How to Dance*—and it was one of the winners in a school contest. The prize was reading my story to kindergartners. I still remember their excited faces as I turned each page, and it was right then and there that I realized this writing and reading thing was a pretty cool deal.

Oddly enough, my PE teacher at the time, Mr. Phillips, taught me an invaluable lesson about perseverance, and the experience stayed with me during years of writing rejections. Trampolines were still allowed in gym class back then, and I was having a rough time mastering a flip. During one attempt, I knocked my knees into my face and got a bloody nose. Before Mr. Phillips let me go to the nurse, he insisted I try one more flip, telling me that if I didn't, I'd never get on the trampoline again. And that was the time I did it. It's often that last time, just when you're about to give up, that you succeed.

Heaps of gratitude to my fairy godmother and agent, Alyssa Eisner Henkin; my editors, Fiona Simpson and Tricia Lin; as well as the entire team at Aladdin, including Hugo Santos for the awesome cover design. A million thanks to ace librarian Sherri Bolen for her constant support; teacher Jenna Bolen for sharing her classroom philosophies with me; the inspiring, wonderful group of writers at the 2016 middle-grade retreat at the Writing Barn in Austin, Texas; and the countless bloggers, teachers, librarians, fellow authors, friends, and readers who share their love of books every day.

And, always, to Ben, Rachel, Sam, and Cassie, who never fail to keep me afloat amidst all the craziness.

Find out how and why

ETHAN MARCUS STOOD UP !

MICHELE WEBER HURWITZ

Middle school is hard.

Solving cases for the FBI is even harder. Doing both at the same time—well, that's just crazy. But that doesn't stop Florian Bates! Get to know the only kid who hangs out with FBI agents *and* international criminals.